The Naughty List

The Naughty List*

Written by Michael Fry and Bradley Jackson
Illustrated by Michael Fry

HARPER
An Imprint of HarperCollins*Publishers*

The Naughty List

For information address HarperCollins Children's Books, a division of HarperCollins Publishers, 195 Broadway, New York, NY 10007.
www.harpercollinschildrens.com

Library of Congress Cataloging-in-Publication Data
Fry, Michael, (date) author, illustrator.
The naughty list / written by Michael Fry and Bradley Jackson ; illustrated by Michael Fry. — First edition.
pages cm
Summary: "Twelve-year-old Bobbie travels to the North Pole to remove her brother from Santa's unimpeachable Naughty List in this Christmas adventure"— Provided by publisher.
ISBN 978-0-06-235475-4 (hardback)
[1. Christmas—Fiction. 2. Santa Claus—Fiction. 3. Humorous stories.] I. Jackson, Bradley, author. II. Title.
PZ7.F9234Nau 2015 2014047808
[Fic]—dc23 CIP
AC

Typography by Rick Farley and David Neuhaus
17 18 19 CG/RRDH 10 9 8 7 6 5 4
❖
First Edition

To Dad, who never followed through on his threat to make me walk home if I spilled ice cream in the car.—MF
To Jake, Scarlet, Luke, Naomi, and Olivia . . . don't forget there's magic.—BJ

Foreword

Magic stinks.

It's true.

If you're lying awake at night hoping something magical happens to you, you're going to be in for a rude surprise.

There are no unicorns or rainbows or that sparkly tinkling sound when that perky, annoying fairy taps her wand. Nope. Everything sounds like a chorus of Auto-Tuned farm animals. And not the cute ones.

How does it feel? Like you've eaten six bags of macaroni-and-cheese dust washed down with a quart of maple syrup while jumping rope for twelve hours.

And it really does stink. You know that gross cheese your grandmother serves with the crackers that expired in 1987? It's like that. TIMES INFINITY!

Maybe it's just me. Maybe it's different for other kids. Or maybe stinky magic is what you get when you try as hard as you can to ruin Christmas.

Like *I* did.

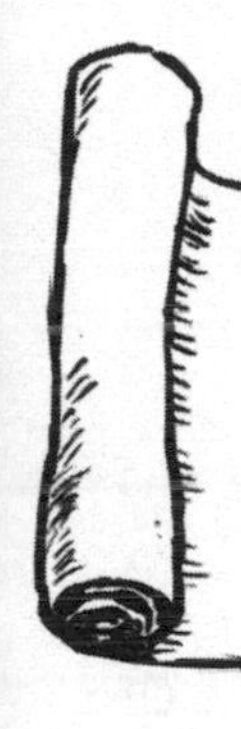

Chapter One

My name is Bobbie Mendoza and my favorite color is black.

Black goes with everything.

Even me.

These days it's about the only thing that does.

The stupid antique dolls over my bed don't. The stupid dress Mom made me wear for picture day doesn't. And the stupid HOT PINK cast I've had on my broken wrist for the last two weeks totally doesn't!

I wanted a black cast.

I never get what I want.

I want to skip being twelve and go straight to twenty-two. I want to eat pizza for breakfast, floss just once a week, and stay up past nine thirty. But most of all I want our house NOT to be the 24/7-Inflatable-Dead-Eyed-Zombie-Santa-on-the-Roof House.

He's been up there for ALMOST AN ENTIRE YEAR!

I wasn't always like this. I wasn't always so angry about everything. I was a normal kid. Not a girly girl exactly, but a regular girl who liked regular stuff. Stuff like waffle-pops (they're better frozen), painting my little brother's toes black while he's asleep, and winning the tristate-area spelling bee.

And I LOVED Christmas.

My favorite part was when Dad and I dressed up our dog, Maggie, like an elf. It was our thing. Every year we'd get more elaborate. Last year was the best.

But not anymore.

Someone left for the North Dakota oil boom and never bothered to take down all the Christmas decorations and someone else is too busy going back to work and someone else is obsessed with Christmas and wants Zombie Santa to stay up forever and someone else won't go on the roof because there's no protection from alien mind-reading rays that turn your brain to cheese.

It's embarrassing! And no one cares! Not my absent dad. Or my always-working mom. Or my freakishly weird Santa-suit-wearing six-year-old brother. Or my we-don't-say-"crazy"-we-say-"different" uncle.

You can die of embarrassment, you know. It's a thing. I read about it online.

Only I didn't die. I just sat in my room and tried to ignore Zombie Santa. Which was hard once most of the air leaked out and he started flapping against my window like the world's saddest flag.

Every. Single. NIGHT!

I didn't lose it right away. First, I did what I always do when I'm freaking out—I motorboat lip hummed "America the Beautiful" to myself. Sure, it's stupid, but somehow it always calms me down. Not this time.

I tried to be brave. I knew things were tough with Dad away and Mom working. That's why every time Mom would ask if I was okay, I'd lie and say, "Fine."

Because deep down I knew that Dad needed this job and Mom needed to work and Tad was just going through a phase . . . AND it was totally just a stupid blow-up Santa. Even if it really, really bugged me that no one could see it. REALLY, REALLY BUGGED ME.

For a while I yelled. And screamed. And did handstands while yelling and screaming.

No response. It was like I was invisible. No. Wait. It wasn't *like* I was invisible. I *was* invisible.

Finally, a couple of weeks before Christmas, after months of Sad Flag Santa flapping against my window, I'd had enough.

I was in the middle of one of those riding-an-Italian-speaking-dragon-while-eating-spaghetti dreams when all of sudden . . .

Zombie Santa attacked!

Actually he didn't really attack. A strong gust of wind blew him through the window. But at three in the morning, in the middle of a riding-a-dragon-while-eating-spaghetti dream, you're not exactly thinking straight.

I snapped. I'd had enough. North Pole Fats was going down. Only he didn't go down alone.

We both did.

Christmas threw me off a roof! Christmas BULLIED ME!

Later, after the pink cast and a lot more lying about how fine I was, I remembered the anti-bullying assembly at school and the fourth thing you do when you're being bullied:

1. TELL AN ADULT.
2. DON'T FIGHT BACK.
3. RUN!
4. IGNORE THE BULLY.

So that's what I did.

I decided to ignore Christmas.

I would not sing any Christmas carols. I would not drink any hot chocolate. I would not partake in any good tidings. And I most certainly would not buy or accept any presents. No exceptions.

What Christmas?

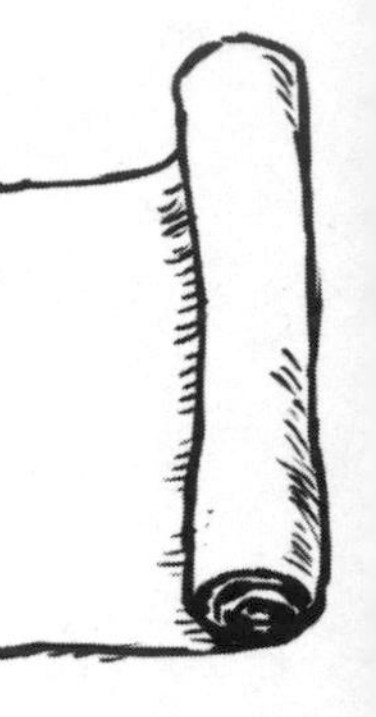

Chapter Two

"You're doing what?" asked Mom from across the dinner table.

"She's ignoring Christmas," said Tad, wearing one of his seven Santa suits. "She thinks it's bullying her."

I could explain (while doing a handstand), but it wouldn't make any difference. They don't understand. No one does.

"That doesn't even make sense," said Mom.

"It makes perfect sense to me," said Uncle Dale.

This should be good.

Not bad.

Uncle Dale continued, "She's ignoring that which causes her pain. Like I'm ignoring this meat loaf."

Mom eyed Uncle Dale. "What's wrong with the meat loaf?"

Uncle Dale didn't say anything. He didn't have to. We all knew what was wrong: Dad didn't make it.

Dad's meat loaf is epic. He makes it from scratch with caramelized onions and his supersecret special BBQ sauce instead of ketchup. It's so awesome, we don't call it meat loaf. We call it meat cake. Once when we were low on cash, Dad served it on my birthday.

No one minded.

Especially not me.

Mom glared at Uncle Dale. She didn't say anything. She knew better than to argue with a man wearing a spaghetti strainer on his head.

Uncle Dale is my dad's younger brother. He used to be a lawyer. And a sock-puppet ventriloquist. And a rodeo clown. And a plumber. He's always had a tough time sticking to one job.

According to Dad, something strange happened to him when he was young. But no one talks about it.

Uncle Dale moved in last year around the time Dad left. He lives in our basement and runs a website called theyreeverywhere.com. He posts stuff about mind-reading aliens that turn your brain to cheese and Big Foot and even Santa.

Uncle Dale even claims the elves text him. Apparently, one named Phil is superchatty.

Mom gave up on Uncle Dale and turned to me. "Bobbie, Christmas is going to happen in two days whether you ignore it or not."

"It's not going to happen to me."

"You don't want any presents?" asked Tad.

I shook my head.

"Well, Santa's bringing me a 3D Mega Machine!" said Tad.

"Maybe, maybe not," said Uncle Dale, looking at his cell phone. "Phil says Bobbie's lack of belief and/or participation in this year's Christmas festivities could affect the delivery of presents."

"And Phil is an . . . elf?" I asked.

"That's the common term," said Uncle Dale. "Technically, Phil is a trans-dimensional sub-reality sprite-being of diminished height with freakishly tapered ears."

"An elf," I said.

Tad turned to Mom. "Is Uncle Dale really texting an elf?"

"Probably just an old college friend. Don't worry, honey," said Mom.

Uncle Dale looked up from his phone. "Oh, I'd worry. Christmas participation powerfully affects inter-flux holiday energy availability. Santa can't cross the Trans-Dimensional Barrier without a full tank of positive holiday flow-vibe."

I couldn't take it. "That's a complete load of . . ."

Mom said, "No, honey, that's not what—"

Uncle Dale nodded. "That's exactly what it—"

"HOLD IT!" I yelled.

Everyone stopped talking and stared at me. "My ignoring Christmas has nothing to do with whether Santa is going to bring Tad his 3D Whateverit'scalled," I said.

"But Uncle Dale said!" cried Tad.

"Uncle Dale wears a spaghetti strainer on his head!"

"Bobbie!" cried Mom.

"Well, he does!" I said.

Uncle Dale frowned. "It's a modified spaghetti strainer. It keeps them from reading my mind."

"Sure. Whatever," I said. "Listen. Who cares if I ignore Christmas? What I do or don't do has no bearing on ANYTHING!"

Mom looked at me. "That's not true—"

Dale's phone buzzed. "According to Phil . . ."

I rolled my eyes. "Who is an elf!"

"What's wrong with being an elf?" asked Tad. "My teacher, Mrs. Hoselnorp, says everybody has to be somebody and we shouldn't 'scrimitate."

"Discriminate, dear," said Mom.

Tad stared at me. "Wait. You don't think elves are REAL!"

I shook my head. "No, I didn't say . . ."

Uncle Dale stared at me. "Ignoring Christmas? Elf doubt? We're not filling Santa's tank here, Bobbie."

Tad pointed at me. "Mom! Make Bobbie fill Santa's tank!"

Mom said, "Bobbie, work with me here! You're the big sister. Please. Act your age."

All I wanted to do was ignore Christmas. Which seemed pretty reasonable when you consider Christmas ATTACKED me! But no one was listening to me—probably because it's hard to hear an invisible person.

Christmas was bullying me again. So I decided to follow rule number three of the anti-bullying list: RUN!

"MOM!" yelled Tad.

"Bobbie!" yelled Mom.

I was already halfway up the stairs.

Later, after the part of my brain that thinks last decided to talk to the part of my brain that thinks first, I thought maybe I'd ruined Christmas for my little brother.

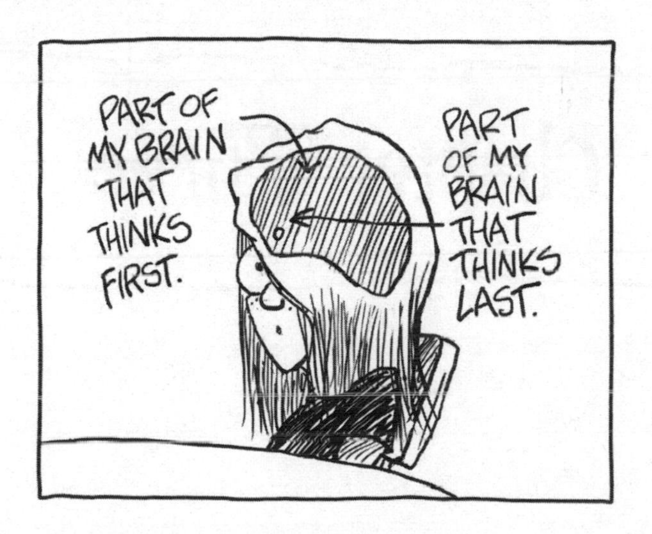

Little did I know, I was just getting started.

Chapter Three

Mom let me stew in my room for a while. She knew I needed some time before her Mom-sense would have any effect on me. Mom-sense is like common sense, only it smells better.

I was staring at my cast, wishing I had laser-beam eyes to burn it off, when I noticed Mom at the door.

"Why haven't you let anyone sign your cast?"

I didn't say anything.

"Is it a part of this whole ignore-Christmas thing?"

BINGO.

She grabbed a pen off my desk, sat down next to me on the bed, and wrote on my cast. I didn't look because I knew she wanted me to look.

"Honey, I know you're angry," she said. "But you can't take it out on Tad. He needs Christmas. With everything we have going on right now he needs to believe in something.

"I guess you're not going to talk to me?" Mom said.

I stared at my shoes.

"That's okay, you'll talk when you're ready," she added.

After she left, I looked at my cast.

Ugh. I keep forgetting she's a Jedi-mom.

After an hour of staring at the ketchup stain on my bedroom ceiling from when Tad and I played splatter tag, I remembered something important.

I got up and went downstairs. Just outside the kitchen I stopped. I could hear Mom talking to Dad over video chat.

Mom said, "I know. Bobbie will be crushed. By the way, she now hates Christmas."

I don't hate Christmas. I'm ignoring Christmas. Big difference.

"What? She loves Christmas," said Dad.

"She thinks Christmas attacked her when she fell off the roof, so now she's getting even," Mom explained.

Not getting even. IGNORING. See! Nobody listens.

"That doesn't sound like her," said Dad.

"And your brother isn't helping the situation with his . . . you know, theories."

"Yeah. Dale's . . . you know, Dale. But he gets even more Dale around Christmas."

"It's not just him. It's this whole situation," said Mom. "You gone. Me working all the time. Bobbie's just acting out."

"Maybe I should come home after all."

YES! YES!

"No. We can't afford it," said Mom. "She'll be fine. Now, what about the video-game thingy that Tad wants?"

"Are you kidding? Bobbie's broken wrist really set us back. Isn't there something else we can get him?"

What? My . . . wrist?

"That's all he wants," said Mom.

"I'm working as many shifts as they'll allow."

"Same here," said Mom.

"Can't we just get him a new sweater or something?"

I'd heard enough.

Not only had I ruined Tad's night, but my stupid broken wrist had blown any chance of him getting a 3D Mega Machine!

Is my ignoring Christmas really messing up everyone's Christmas? Could Uncle Dale be right?

Nah.

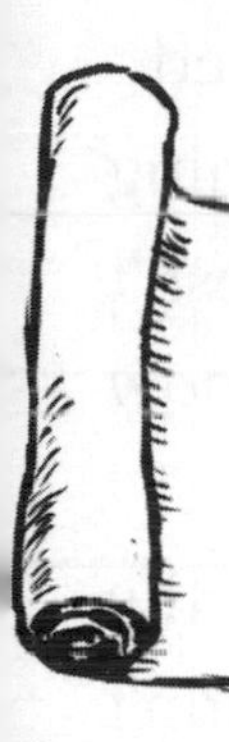

Chapter Four

I walked back into my room in a daze. Tad was waiting for me.

"John Noodlehorn said Santa's just a fake thing made up by adults. And tonight you were acting like he wasn't real either," he said.

Ignoring Christmas is one thing. Destroying Tad's Christmas? No way!

I was desperate for a way to change the subject when I noticed a letter in his hand. "What's that?" I asked.

"It's a letter to Santa. I wrote down the only thing I really want in the whole world and if Santa doesn't bring it to me then I'll know he's not real and I'll know you're right and we can ignore Christmas together."

This didn't sound like Tad. It didn't sound like the same kid who'd never met a pile of leaves he didn't want to dive-bomb or the little boy who was convinced that ants pooped glitter.

You know that feeling when you watch a sad movie and it's like a lizard's crawling up your throat and your nose starts to tingle and your eyes get all sweaty?

That's how I felt.

I wiped my eyes with my cast.

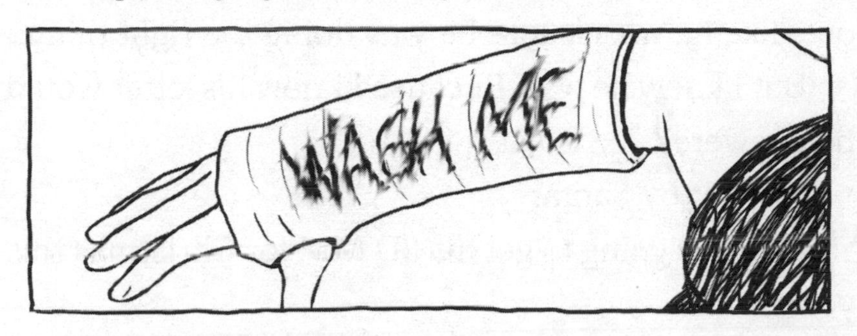

Tad got up and walked toward the door. "I'm going to go put this in the mailbox."

A few seconds later I heard the front door open. I peered out the window and looked down.

Tad walked toward the mailbox. He looked nervous, like he wasn't sure he was doing the right thing.

But I knew he was. Because I knew his letter would be answered.

But not by Santa.

Tad was going to get his 3D MM for Christmas this year.

Somehow, someway, I would get it for him.

I just had to figure out how.

Chapter Five

I knew the 3D MM wasn't cheap. Back in my room, I checked the price online.

I quickly checked my sock bank.

Okay, so buying one was out of the question. There had to be another way. Wait. Could I raise the money?

No chance.

I couldn't buy it. I couldn't raise the money. What else?

Christmas was doomed. I was ready to give up when I heard Uncle Dale downstairs yelling at the TV.

"Garbage! Total garbage!" he shouted. "The suits are wrong. The workshop is wrong. There is no reindeer sauna. It's an established fact that elves work flex-time! Outrageous!"

I poked my head out of my room just as Uncle Dale was about to head down to his basement lair.

"What are you watching?" I asked.

"Trash!" snapped Uncle Dale. "It's nothing like that!" he shouted as he slammed the door behind him.

With nothing better to do, I went downstairs, sat down, and punched info on the remote.

Uncle Dale was right. It was total garbage.

I was about to turn the TV off when a commercial for Toyopolis came on.

And just like that I had a much better plan.

That's when I realized that to save Tad's Christmas I was going to have to stop ignoring Christmas and embrace my inner ho-ho-ho.

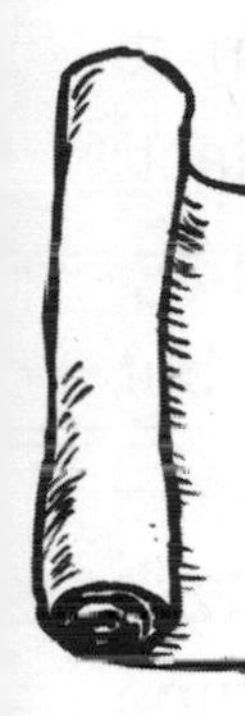

Chapter Six

I woke up Christmas Eve morning and suited up. I'm not into clothes. But even I know Santa is so totally not fashion forward.

The only other living thing (besides Tad) I've ever seen in red velvet and white trim was Jack, our neighbor Mrs. Stankly's miniature Doberman.

Don't get me started on Santa's stupid hat with that ridiculous bell sewn onto the end. And the beard? You'd think Mrs. Claus would put a razor on her Christmas list. Or at least a chain saw.

The only practical thing Santa has going for him is that sack. It's Tad's favorite Santa accessory—in fact, when he was younger he'd use it as a sleeping bag. Which is pretty weird when you think about it . . . but I wasn't thinking about that.

What I was thinking about was how a Santa sack would be perfect for stashing a 3D Mega Machine when I won the contest.

Because . . . I was going to win.

As I entered Toyopolis, I figured who else besides me is going to wear high-water Santa capri pants and risk the shame of total global embarrassment?

I had no idea the line for total global embarrassment would be so long.

There were Santas everywhere! There were Cat-Juggling Unicycle Santas.

There were Afro-Elvis Santas.

There were Star Wars Santas . . .

And there was one guy who obviously didn't listen very closely to the commercial.

There was no way I could compete. They all had awesome costumes and all I had was a . . .

To make matters worse all the contestants had to perform on a small stage. I don't perform. I'm not really that good at anything. Except, you know, being invisible. But that doesn't work so well in front of an audience.

As I stood last in a long line of freakishly weird Santas, I thought, what could I possibly do that nobody else here can do?

No. I mean, yes, I'm probably the only one here who can spell "curmudgeon." But no, that's not going to win a 3D MM.

Wait. I know that sound. I make that sound. That's the motorboat lip humming sound. I motorboat lip hum like nobody's business. That's what I can do! I can be the Motorboat Lip Humming Santa!

I turned around to thank whoever had made the sound, but no one was there.

Weird. But not as weird as Pop-N-Lock Santa "performing" onstage.

After the paramedics rolled Pop-N-Lock Santa away, it was my turn. I climbed onstage and stood next to the judge, local radio DJ Sleez-Bone.

I don't listen to Sleez-Bone on the radio. I heard somewhere stupidity is contagious.

Sleez-Bone said, "So, kid, what's your Santa angle?"

"I hum," I said.

"Hum?"

"I motorboat lip hum."

"You what?"

I set down the Santa Sack because every true artist needs both hands when they're about to paint a masterpiece.

I gripped the microphone, closed my eyes, and nailed the best "Star Spangled Banner" Motorboat Lip Hum ever.

It was epic. I knew it was epic because everyone was speechless. When you hear true motorboat lip humming genius there's nothing to say, except . . .

Panda doesn't even rhyme with Santa! Tad was not getting a 3D MM. Christmas was doomed. AGAIN!

As I stepped off the stage in shame, I noticed two strange little kids wearing their own Santa suits sitting in a cart holding what looked like . . . Is that Tad's Santa sack?

They must have grabbed it when I set it down.

"Hey! That's my brother's!" I shouted. I ran over to grab it when . . .

. . . a different strange little kid in a Santa suit grabbed the sack. What is going on?

When I turned back to the cart, the first two tiny thieves were gone. Where'd they go?

It was chaos. Strange little kids in Santa suits were everywhere playing keep-away with Tad's Santa sack.

Just because I couldn't win a 3D MM for Tad didn't mean I was gonna let a bunch of creepy Santa sneaks steal Tad's favorite accessory.

There's this part in *Ninja Santa 2: Escape from the South Pole* where Rudolph dangles from a cliff by his harness. (He was pushed over the cliff by Slasher, Dasher's evil twin. I know. It's stupid.) Ninja Santa runs in EPIC ULTRA SLOW MOTION to catch Rudolph before he falls.

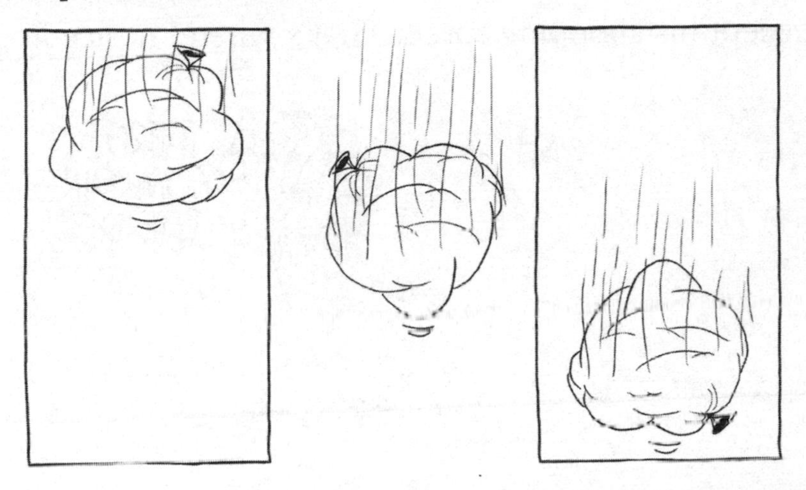

That's exactly how I felt as I dove for the sack. (Except with a lot fewer plot holes and cheesy special effects.)

But still . . . it was pretty awesome.

I slid to a halt behind the crowd of Santa freaks huddled in front of the stage watching Panda Santa accept his shopping spree. That's when I noticed . . .

Before I could figure out what it was, one of the strange-looking little kids stood on the shoulders of one of the Santa freaks, then pointed at me, and yelled in a high-pitched, almost robotic voice . . .

As I walked away, I started to think maybe all those strange-looking little kids weren't kids at all.

"Where do you think you're going?" said a super-scary deep voice behind me.

I turned around and looked up.

The Santa sack? But there's nothing in there but crumpled-up newspapers.

I couldn't breathe.

How in the world did the 3D Mega Machine get inside?! Did one of those weird toddler Santas slip it in? What's the food like in prison? Do they make you eat lima beans? I hate lima beans. But before any of my questions could be answered . . .

Someone set off the store fire alarm, which set off the sprinklers, which set off the Santas . . .

The Santa scrum carried me outside the store, where I was able to slip away during all the confusion that, you know, normally comes with a Santa scrum.

I ducked behind the store and slowly peered inside the bag. My heart skipped a beat. And then five more. Did I just save Tad's Christmas?

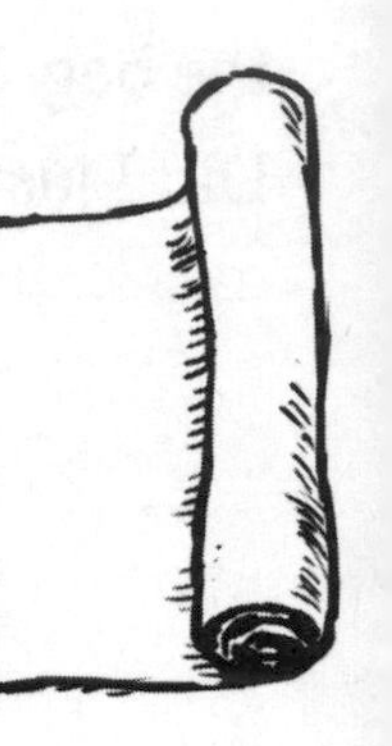

Chapter Seven

Wait. But didn't I just steal? Am I a thief?

YES	NO
1. IT'S IN MY SACK.	1. I DIDN'T PUT IT IN THERE.
2. I DIDN'T PAY FOR IT.	2. DO I HAVE A SUPER THIN MOUSTACHE THAT TWIRLS UP AT THE END?
3. I FEEL SORT OF QUEASY LIKE THAT TIME I TOOK FIVE EXTRA MINTS AFTER DINNER AT EL POLLO LOCO.	3. DO I HAVE A HYENA-PITCHED EVIL LAUGH?

I peered around the corner and spotted the security guard looking for me.

I could see it in his eyes. I was a thief.

And there's no way he'd believe I didn't actually steal it.

There were only two things I could do. Turn myself in.

OR . . .

And that's when that creepy Christmas song started playing on loudspeakers outside the store.

He sees you when you're sleeping. He knows when you're awake.

Hold it.

First of all . . . Santa's *watching* you sleep? That's seriously creepy.

You're telling me Santa's just sitting in front of a bank of screens waiting for kids to mess up so he can smirk and snicker and KILL their Christmas with a check of his pen?!

C'mon, who does that?

Second of all—the song's about a Naughty List? Seriously?

Here I was, considering doing a sort of naughty

thing, BUT . . . if I "stole" the gift it would be for a good reason, which Santa couldn't know 'cause all he'd see was the naughty thing and not the supernice reason behind it.

Which is exactly why the Naughty List—IF a Naughty List existed—couldn't be fair or accurate or . . .

That's when it hit me: There's no Naughty List. But there is a little kid who deserves a great Christmas. And I'm going to give it to him.

Then I'm going to pay the store back. Somehow.

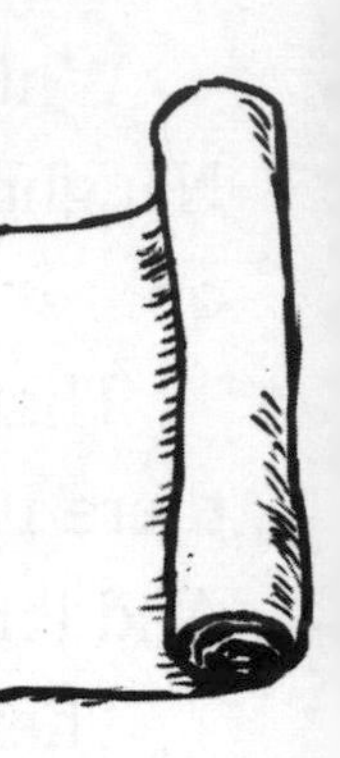

Chapter Eight

After I'd mentally devised the best way to pay back Toyopolis . . .

BOBBIE'S FIVE-POINT REPAYMENT PLAN

1. WITHDRAW MONEY FROM SOCK BANK.
2. SPELLING BEE CHAMPION ENDORSEMENTS.
3. MOTORBOAT LIP HUM GREATEST HITS ALBUM.
4. SELL SPLEEN.
5. GET JOB.

. . . I headed home. You know how you walk into your house millions of times with no one around? But somehow when you try to sneak in, EVERYONE is there.

"Now, snow angels, that's a different story," said Uncle Dale.

"But what about Frosty?" Tad asked.

"You mean General J. R. Frostman Jr.?" said Uncle Dale. "Greatest snowman leader since his father. Snowmen are the Spartans of the North Pole. They're fiercely protective of the Trans-Dimensional Barrier."

"How do you know all this stuff?" Tad asked.

Uncle Dale pointed to his head. "Cheese-free."

I ducked down behind the hedge. Which was hard with our neighbor Mr. Wilcox's creepy garden gnomes staring at me from their weird tropical island display.

I sized up the situation. I couldn't walk past Tad and Uncle Dale holding a bag with a sopping wet Santa suit and a "gift." I was going to have to stash it somewhere for later. But where?

"Wait," I said to myself. "Is that gnome pointing to the grass hut? That's it! I can hide the game in the hut!"

And that's what I did.

Afterward I set the fallen gnome back on his feet.

“What are you doing?” interrupted Uncle Dale.

“Um . . . one of the gnomes got knocked over and I . . .”

Uncle Dale pointed at the disco gnome. “That one?”

I turned to look. “Yeah. How did you . . .”

Uncle Dale didn’t answer. He just slowly nodded and walked away. “You’d better come in before your mom gets home and figures out you’ve been gone.”

“Gone? I haven’t been . . .”

I had no idea what was up with Uncle Dale and I didn’t have time to figure it out.

I was about to have much bigger problems.

Chapter Nine

It took forever before I was able to sneak back out to get the game. First we had Christmas Eve dinner (leftover meat loaf), then Tad insisted we all watch the Ninja Santa Christmas Special on TV.

Then Mom made me take a shower AND wash my hair. Afterward, completely inconsiderate of my needs, she insisted that that night, out of all nights, would be a good night to bond.

Moms—it's always about them.

Just before she left she hit me with one of her Jedi-mom stares.

"I have something for you," she said. "I know you don't want any gifts for Christmas, but this technically isn't a gift. It's more of a re-gift. My mom gave it to me."

She took a locket on a chain out of her pocket and put it around my neck. "This is for the next time you forget who *you* are. It's to remind you that you matter."

She kissed me on the neck and left. I inspected the locket. There was an inscription: Open locket in case of identity theft.

I opened it. Inside was a mirror.

Jedi-mom strikes again.

I pretended to go to bed. After about an hour I went to my door and listened. Silence.

I put on my sneakers, snuck downstairs, and went out the front door.

I quietly tiptoed to the grass hut with a sly grin on my face. I had this wired. This was going to be the best Christmas ever.

Not so fast.

Did Uncle Dale take it? Did Tad? But before I had time to throw a proper fit . . .

"What the . . . Tad?"

I heard Mom shout from inside the house, "Tad? What happened?"

Something must have exploded inside the house. As I sprinted back I could hear Uncle Dale frantically yelling, "I've secured the perimeter! Everyone to the Safe Room!"

The Safe Room is a boarded-up space under the basement stairs stocked with everything Uncle Dale needs to survive an alien apocalypse.

I didn't have time to deal with Uncle Dale. I ran as fast as I could up the stairs. I stopped just outside Tad's room, where they couldn't see me.

Tad was holding the game console. He had blue dye all over his face. But how did the game get to his room?

"It was just sitting on my bed!" he cried.

"And how did it get there?" asked Mom.

"Santa put it there!"

Mom's mouth shrunk to the size of a shriveled raisin. You can always tell how angry Mom is by how tight her lips get in comparison to dried fruit.

"Well, I sure didn't buy it. Did you take my credit card and buy this online?"

"No! It was Santa! It had to be!"

"T-minus three minutes until Safe Room lock-down!" yelled Uncle Dale from downstairs. "S'mores are in the microwave. Repeat. S'mores are in the microwave."

Mom shook her head at Tad. "We can't afford this. It's going straight back to wherever it came from."

"But Mom—" he started.

Mom wasn't done. "And if this is what you think is acceptable behavior then maybe we should take a page out of your sister's playbook and all ignore Christmas this year."

Tad's eyes watered. His mouth quivered. His lip did that stick-out thing that only little kids can make work.

Suddenly it didn't matter that there wasn't any Naughty List, or Santa, or elves, or that whole not-getting-to-play-reindeer-games thing.

It didn't matter because reality has no chance against fantasy . . .

. . . when you believe.

And Tad was a believer. He believed in Christmas. And now his Christmas was ruined.

Unless . . . I stepped up and told Mom the truth.

I cleared my voice, breathed deep, and took a step into Tad's room . . . and that's when I smelled something seriously gross.

Refried beans?

Chapter Ten

Tad and Mom were frozen in place. I could move. Sort of. It was like the air was denser, but only in some places.

I didn't feel so hot. For a second I thought I was gonna hurl dinner chunks all over the carpet. But then it passed.

"What exactly do you think you are doing?"

"Chill, dude."

Voices. Not Tad. Not Mom. Not Uncle Dale. "Who's there?" I asked.

"Chill? Dude? You know how I loathe hipster-speak."

Both voices were super high-pitched, like dolphins on helium. One voice had an English accent and the other sounded . . . I don't know . . . regular-ish? But where were they coming from?

"You wouldn't know a hipster if it came up and tattooed your butt."

I scanned the room. All I could see was a dim sliver of light under Tad's closet door.

"I'll thank you to leave my bottom out of this!"

The voices were coming from Tad's closet!

"Look, I didn't have a choice. She was going to con—"

"You're the two strange-looking little . . . GNOMES!" I screamed.

"Gnomes?! That is truly insulting," said the dumpy one.

The thin one shook his head. "So I guess all short, squat, pointy-eared, trans-dimensional sprite-beings are the same to you people. It never changes."

I backed away. "What is going ON?"

"Oh dear, she's become hysterical," said Dumpy.

Skinny put up his hands. "Let's not freak out here."

"You . . . you were in the . . . the toy store and in Mr. Wilcox's g-garden next door!" I stammered.

"Quite observant," said the dumpy one.

"You're stalking me!" I cried.

Dumpy shook his head. "Observing. From a respectful distance. Stalking implies harm. We mean no harm."

"Elves?" I whispered. "Santa's elves?"

They both nodded slowly.

"Santa . . . is . . . real?"

They looked at one another. Then Dumpy looked back at me and nodded. "Yes, my dear Bobbie, there is a Santa Claus."

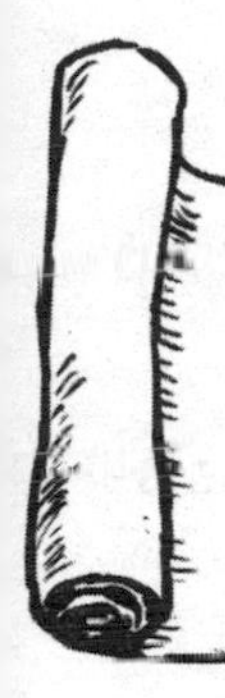

Chapter Eleven

I stared with my mouth open for a few seconds.

"You probably have a few questions?" said Skinny.

I had a few THOUSAND questions! From the basic, if Santa is real then how does he deliver presents to billions of kids in one night to how do you maintain a toy factory at the North Pole during a period of climate change. . . .

But I didn't ask those questions. I started simple. "What're you doing here?"

"An excellent question, but first, I think it's best if we introduce ourselves," said Dumpy. "I'm Gumdrop and this cheeky lad is Phil."

Phil took a deep bow. "Yo."

If I'm dreaming all this, why couldn't I come up with better names?

Gumdrop said, "We are here to offer our assistance."

"Assistance?"

"Your brother?" said Phil as he pointed to Tad still frozen across the room. "And his recent placement on the Naughty List?"

"Wait. That's not really real," I said. "Is it?"

"As real as two tiny dudes standing here with bells on," said Phil.

Phil stared at Gumdrop. "You move like you've got a lump of coal up your butt."

"Silence!" yelled Gumdrop. "Where was I?"

"The Naughty List," I said.

"Yes. Quite. You see, now that Tad's on the list he can't get off without—"

"He didn't steal the game, I did!" I cried. "I mean, I sort of stole it but not really. I mean, yes, technically I left the store with it, but not on purpose."

"We know. We were there," said Gumdrop.

"Yeah, and thanks for ratting me out to that security guard," I reminded them.

They both gulped. "I'm afraid that wasn't us, darling," said Gumdrop.

"Oh yeah, then who was it?" I asked.

"We'll get to that, kid, but first let's focus on baby brother for now. Don't you want him to have a holly jolly Christmas?" asked Phil.

"Of course. Just take him off the list and put me on instead," I said.

"It's not that simple," said Gumdrop. "This list isn't compiled by us. It's . . . well, it's complicated."

Phil interrupted. "The Naughty List is handled by the Watcher. The Watcher is really good at watching. Not so good at seeing."

"The Watcher?" I asked.

"Too many children," said Gumdrop. "The entire process has become automated."

"What about Santa?"

"That's a whole other story," said Gumdrop.

"Then just tell the Watcher to take Tad off and put me on."

"We can't do that. But you can," said Phil.

"WHAT?!"

"There's an appeals process," said Gumdrop. "Hardly ever used . . . well, never used. But it does exist."

"You and Tad must petition for an appeal," Phil added.

"Stop!" I yelled. "Just stop. This is ridiculous! As much as I want Tad to have a merry Christmas I'm not about to go off with two weird-looking crazies just so he can have some stupid video-game system!"

"I think it's time to show her the letter," said Phil.

Gumdrop nodded as Phil reached into his coat and handed me Tad's letter to Santa.

"How did you . . . ?" I started.

"It's a copy; the real version is in the Holiday Hall of Requests," said Gumdrop.

"Read it," said Phil.

I rolled my eyes as I opened Tad's letter.

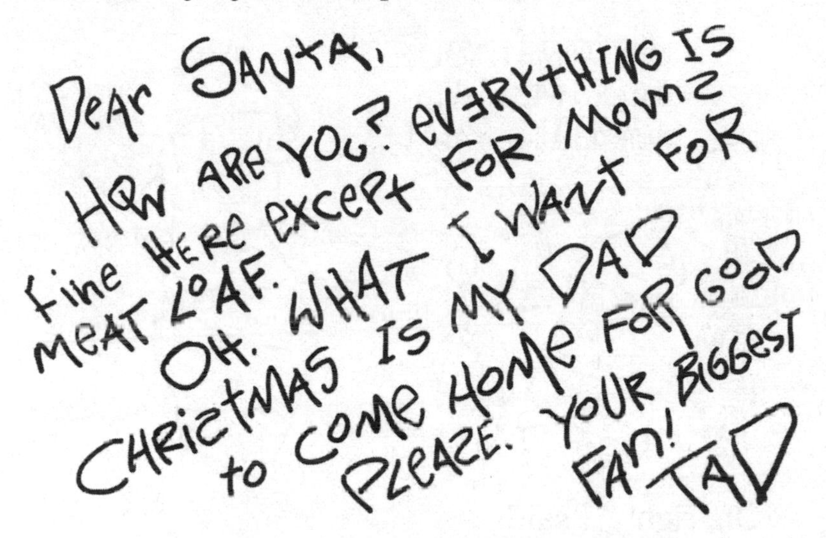

Dear Santa,
How are you? Everything is fine here except for Momz meat loaf. Oh. What I want for Chriztmas is my Dad to come home for good pleaze.
Your Biggest Fan!
Tad

"If you don't get Tad off the Naughty List his wish will never come true," said Phil.

I felt dizzy. I steadied myself, turned, and looked back at frozen Mom and Tad. Then I turned around to the two elves. "Dad could come home?"

"Only if you win the appeal," said Gumdrop.

"An appeal? Like in a court? I don't know anything about courts?"

"But I do."

I turned around. Uncle Dale was standing at the door holding a plate of four s'mores. "S'mores, anyone?"

I stared at Uncle Dale. "You're part of all this?"

Uncle Dale nodded. "I haven't been briefed on the details. But yes, Phil, Gumdrop, and I are acquainted."

"Oh, right," I said.

WHAM!

"What was that?"

"They're here!" said Gumdrop.

"Who's here?"

"No time to explain," said Phil. "We have to go. We have to go NOW!"

"But what about Tad and Mom?"

“They’ll be fine. The group downstairs is after us, not them,” said Gumdrop as he opened the closet door.

“A submarine?” I asked.

“How else would we get to the North Pole?” asked Phil.

“I don’t know,” I said. “Magic?”

As we all fled into the closet Gumdrop looked back at me and yelled, “Magic, my dear, has its limitations.”

Chapter Twelve

I followed the elves into Tad's closet—past the penciled lines of Tad's rising height, past his three other gross-smelling Santa Suits, and way, way past the point where any six-year-old's closet should go.

When I stopped, the closet was gone, replaced by a creaky wooden dock leading to a small submarine. I looked around as the icy winds whipped my hair into a frozen frenzy.

"In serious danger! Now GET ON BOARD!" shouted Uncle Dale with that angry tone he uses only to yell at reality shows like *My Big Fat Bigfoot Neighbor.*

A hatch on top of the sub flew open. A bearded elf wider than he was tall popped his head out and yelled, "Hurry up, humans! That is unless you wanna doggy-paddle to the North Pole!"

I asked anyone who would listen. "Will someone

please tell me what's going on?"

"No time! Move!" yelled Phil as he pushed me toward a rusty ladder leading to the hatch.

I was about halfway up when I heard a bright, harsh sound behind me. I turned just in time to see a half dozen of those freaky little evil-smiling elf dudes from the toy store explode out of Tad's closet and onto the dock.

They looked angry. Like they wanted to hurt someone. Mainly me.

"Who the heck are they?" I shouted.

"Nobody important!" yelled Gumdrop as the bearded elf tossed him a long tube of what looked like Christmas wrapping paper.

"Gift wrap?" I asked as Gumdrop aimed the tube at the charging elves like a holiday-themed bazooka.

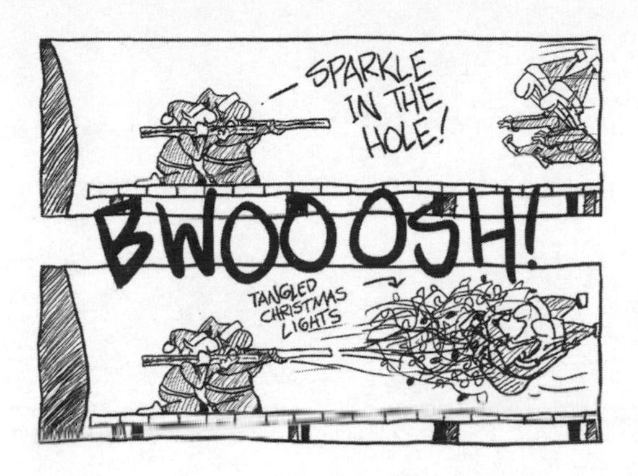

I watched from the sub as the angry elves struggled with the spiderweb of lights only to become more entangled.

"DIVE, DIVE, DIVE!" yelled the bearded elf (who I now dubbed Captain Wide-Beard) as a hand grabbed my leg and yanked me into the darkness below.

Inside, it took my eyes a few seconds to adjust to the red-and-green glow of the instruments. The first thing that came into view was Uncle Dale staring down at me.

At least someone was having fun.

Chapter Thirteen

Other than the fact that it was operated by elves (and smelled like cinnamon), the inside of the sub looked pretty much like what you'd think the inside of a sub would look like.

I was starting to figure out that this wasn't Uncle Dale's first trip to the North Pole. But before I could ask how he knew everybody . . .

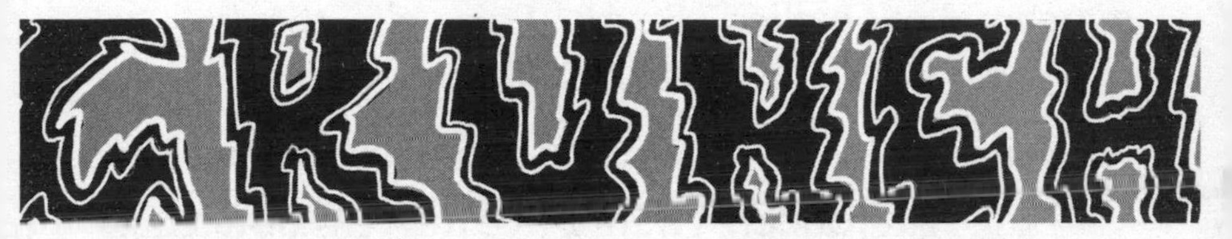

One second I was staring at Uncle Dale. The next I was kissing the deck.

WREEEE

"What's happening?" I shouted over the alarms and sirens.

"Battle stations!" Captain Wide-Beard yelled. "Robo-Narwhals off the starboard bow!"

I picked myself up off the deck and peeked out the nearest porthole.

“I do believe they’re trying to ram us!” shouted Gumdrop.

“If they think we’re gonna lie down like some marshmallow-bellied South Pole elf, they’ve got another thing coming!” shouted Captain Wide-Beard. “Full right rudder! Twenty-five degrees down bubble!”

“Full right rudder! Twenty-five degrees down bubble!” repeated a high-pitched voice.

Both Uncle Dale and I were thrown to the deck again while all the elves kept their footing. I guess being real close to the ground has its advantages.

I looked to Uncle Dale. He was still beaming from ear to ear! “Having fun yet?”

“Are you crazy?” I asked.

“Nope. I’ve just seen stuff most folks wouldn’t believe!”

"They've breached the hull! We're taking on water!" shouted an elf belowdecks.

THINGS YOU DON'T WANT TO HEAR ON A SUBMARINE

1. THEY'VE BREACHED THE HULL.
2. WE'RE TAKING ON WATER.
3. WHO FARTED?

"We're sinking!" cried a different elf.

I turned to Uncle Dale. He suddenly wasn't smiling anymore.

"Everyone! Shut your blowholes!" barked Captain Wide-Beard.

Silence. The only sound was the steady whoosh of water rushing into the sub. That and . . .

Gumdrop went to hug Phil. "Smashing! It's Henrietta to the rescue!"

Phil put his arms up. "What did we say about hugging?"

Gumdrop stopped and stared at his curly shoes. "Apologies."

"We're saved!" cheered the crew.

I waved my arms. "Hello? Henrietta? Singing? Saved? Anyone?"

Phil pointed at the porthole.

"Henrietta's a friend. And a whale. A whale-friend," said Phil.

I stared at him. "Blow your hole? Blow your hole? Blow your hole?"

Gumdrop said, "She prefers her own version. For a marine mammal she's quite creative."

I looked out the porthole again. Henrietta's eye was gone. I couldn't see what happened next. But this is my best guess . . .

Phil and Gumdrop assured me we'd be fine. But the last thing I was . . . was fine. I was as far from fine as you can get.

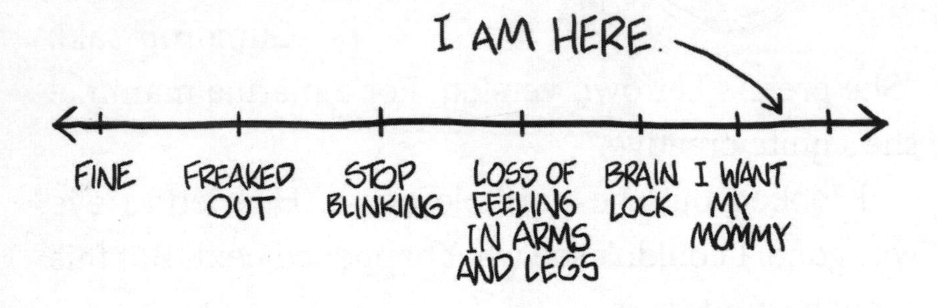

Chapter Fourteen

I shook my head. "Now you're telling me we're inside a singing whale?"

Phil shrugged. "I guess that seems kind of weird, huh?"

Weird? No weirder than an elf-operated submarine, Robo-Narwhals, angry elves, or the Watcher . . . or the fact that no one would tell me . . .

Gumdrop looked at Phil, who looked at Uncle Dale, who looked at the captain, who looked back at Gumdrop, who looked at me. "Can you be more specific, dear?"

"Let's start with the Watcher," I suggested.

Gumdrop looked at Phil. "Oh, bother. Where to begin?"

Phil rolled his eyes. "Try the beginning."

Gumdrop glared at Phil. "Not helping." He turned to me. "As we said back in your brother's room, the Watcher compiles the Naughty List."

"Why?" I asked.

"Have a seat," Phil said. "This could take a while."

BUT AS THE WORLD GREW, CHRISTMAS EXPLODED. THE SUPPLY OF CHEER FROM NICE KIDS COULDN'T KEEP UP. WE NEEDED MORE NICE KIDS. WE NEEDED NAUGHTY KIDS TO TURN NICE.

ENTER THE NAUGHTY LIST.

THE IDEA WASN'T TO PUNISH NAUGHTY KIDS, BUT TO ENCOURAGE THEM TO BE NICE.

MAINTAINING A NAUGHTY LIST REQUIRES WATCHING EVERY CHILD IN THE WORLD IN REAL TIME. TO DO THAT YOU NEED A MACHINE. YOU NEED A...

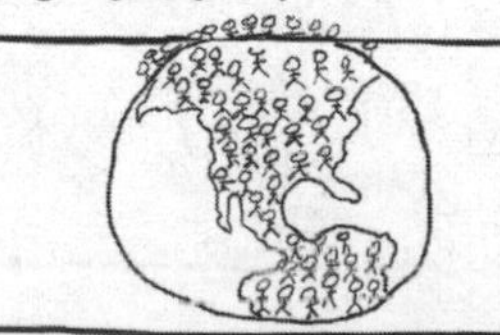

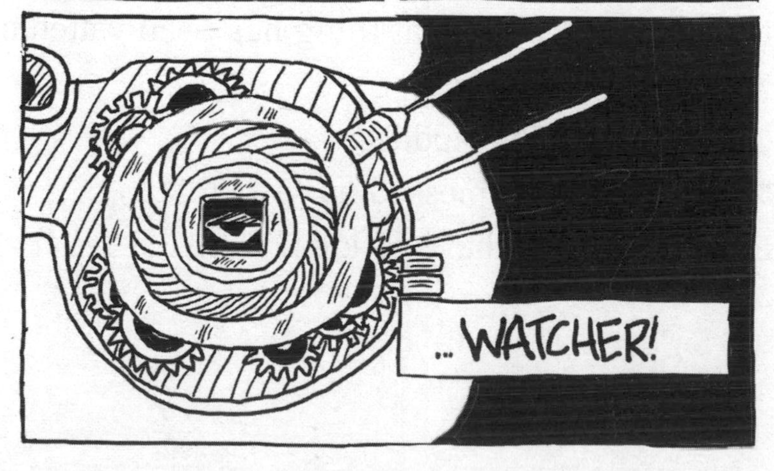

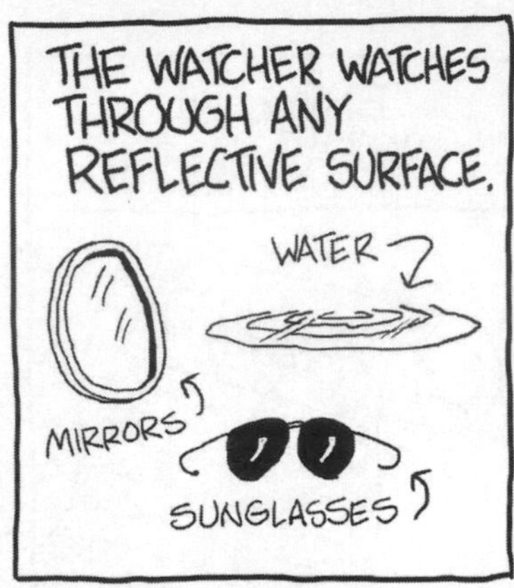

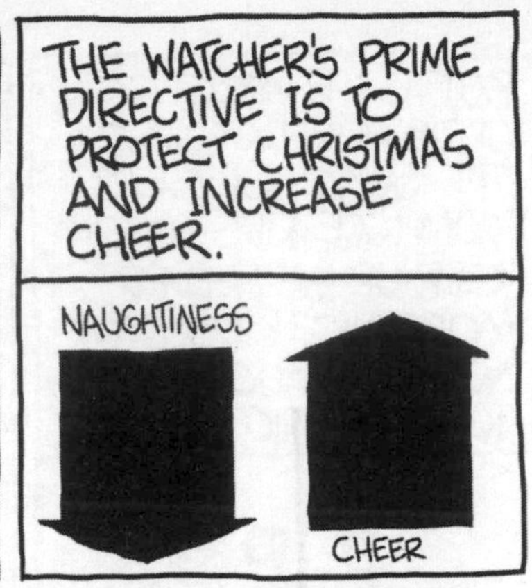

I shook my head. "That thing has been watching me? EVERY SECOND?"

Gumdrop and Phil nodded.

"That is seriously messed up," I said.

Phil sighed. "You have no idea."

Chapter Fifteen

All I could do was stare at my shoes. I felt like Ninja Santa in that scene in *Ninja Santa 4: The Reckoning* when the president tells Ninja Santa that the Easter Bunny and the Tooth Fairy have betrayed him and pledged allegiance to his evil clone.

I looked up. Everyone was staring at me. Phil said, "Way to go, Gumdrop. You blew her mind."

Gumdrop looked worried. "Oh dear, I didn't mean to," he said.

Uncle Dale put his arm around me. "She's fine. I was the same way when I heard the truth and look at me."

I stared at the spaghetti strainer on Uncle Dale's head.

"Okay," I said. "I'm still confused. What about those angry elves? And the Robo-Narwhals? Why were they trying to stop us?"

Phil looked at Gumdrop. "Uh . . . well . . ."

Gumdrop continued, "What he's trying to say is . . . it's . . . well, it's their job."

"Right," said Phil. "They're part of a . . . a force—"

Gumdrop interrupted. "A robot force that protects the Trans-Dimensional Barrier . . ."

"From humans," piped Phil.

"Robots? Those elves? They were robots?" I asked.

"Exactly. Robots. Scary, mean robots," said Phil.

"They're part of a defense system. Humans aren't

supposed to cross the Trans-Dimensional Barrier," said Gumdrop.

"And . . . um . . . we just forgot to tell them you were coming," said Phil.

Gumdrop shrugged. "Oops!"

"Oops?" I said.

Phil raised his hands. "We'll straighten it all out when we get to the North Pole. No worries. Let's just concentrate on getting Tad off the Naughty List."

"So your dad can come home for Christmas," added Gumdrop.

Around the sub all the elves nodded simultaneously.

I shook my head. "Okay. But—"

A low rumble rattled the sub. It sounded like my stomach just after eating Mom's meat loaf.

"It's Henrietta!" yelled Captain Wide-Beard. "She's hurlin' us back to the sea!"

Barfed up by a whale. I can check that off my bucket list.

BOBBIE'S BUCKET LIST

- [ ] 1. BECOME CEO OF WAFFLE POPS INC.
- [ ] 2. LEARN TO PLAY BAGPIPES.
- [ ] 3. SEE THE WORLD'S BIGGEST BALL OF LINT.
- [x] 4. GET BARFED UP BY A WHALE.
- [ ] 5. SWIM WITH THE SQUIDS.

"We must be near the North Pole," said Uncle Dale.

"Already?" I said. "We've only been gone, like, an hour."

Gumdrop said, "We're now in Trans-Dimensional space/time. Distance gets a little . . . um, wiggy."

I looked at Phil.

Phil nodded. "It's a technical term. It means whacked."

The sub lurched forward as Henrietta violently RALPHED us back out to the ocean.

"Candy Cane Reef dead ahead!" cried Captain Wide-Beard.

I looked out the porthole. "Are they dangerous?" I asked.

Captain Wide-Beard nodded. "Edges sharper than a narwhal horn. One swipe will tear this metal hunk in half and send us all to a deep, dark, minty death. Steady as she goes."

I held my breath. It was quiet. Almost too quiet when suddenly . . .

The alarms were sounding again. "ROGUE PEPPERMINT OFF THE PORT BOW!" yelled one of the elves.

"EVASIVE MANEUVERS!" cried Captain Wide-Beard.

The captain yelled, "SURFACE! NOW!"

"But the ice!" cried Uncle Dale.

The force of impact threw my head against a bulk-head. It hurt. A lot. At least until everything went dark. And cold.

Seriously cold.

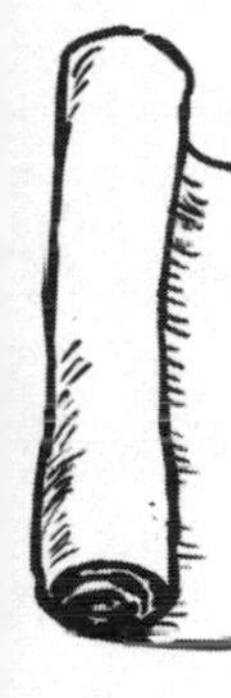

Chapter Sixteen

I'm in my bed. Warm. Asleep. Safe.

"Bobbie?"

"Go away."

"Bobbie, wake up."

"No."

"You have to wake up."

"Leave me alone. I'm in bed. Asleep. Safe."

"BOBBIE, WAKE UP!"

I opened my eyes. I was not in my bed. I was not asleep. I was not safe.

I was being carried across the dark ice in the

middle of a blizzard. There was no sign of the sub or any of the elves.

"DUCK!" yelled an elf voice.

Uncle Dale dove to the ground as something in the air whizzed past our heads.

"Look out!" cried the elf.

Uncle Dale threw himself on top of me. That's when I saw it . . .

I whispered, “What? Was? That?”

“Snow angels!” yelled Uncle Dale.

“Snow what? What the . . . Where? How . . . ?”

“You were knocked out. The sub was sinking. We abandoned ship. Uh-oh. Don’t look!”

I looked.

There were dozens of them—diving and shrieking, their mouths twisted into permanent screams.

AYEEEEEEE

“They don’t look very angelic to me,” I said.

"They're angry," said Uncle Dale. "At you and a million other kids who created and then abandoned them."

Hold on. It's not like anyone warned me.

Suddenly, the shrieking stopped. The Snow Angels disappeared. I figured they finally realized they were being just a tad unreasonable.

I figured wrong.

Out of the swirling blizzard another shrieking wave attacked.

"RUN!" yelled Uncle Dale.

We ran. Which is really hard at the North Pole. You'd think it might be like running across a frozen lake. It's not. It's like running across an ocean that flash froze in the middle of a hurricane.

The angels were almost on us. I looked to my left as one of them dove at one of the elves. He ducked, but not before the angel brushed past his pointy ear, flash freezing the tip.

Not good. Those things have a serious chip on their wings.

"This way!" yelled Uncle Dale.

I followed him between two ice sheets that had collided and formed a deep crevasse. As another angry angel wave rocketed past, we jumped in . . .

and landed on Phil and Gumdrop.

"They'll be back," said Phil.

"Then what?" I asked.

"I don't know," Phil replied.

"You don't know!"

"I'm pretty sure this wasn't part of the plan," Gumdrop added.

"There's a PLAN?"

That's when we saw them. Six snow angels hovered directly above us preparing to attack. I looked at Uncle Dale. Uncle Dale looked at me. Then . . .

"Git behind me, ya wicked white demons!" bellowed a deep voice.

We looked up.

We were saved. But by who? Or what?

Another snow soldier appeared. "General Frostman, the snow freaks are in full retreat."

"Good. Round up this lot and we'll head back to base."

"Yes, sir."

Uncle Dale and I just stood there and stared as the general lit his pipe then pointed at the puddled remains of the snow angel. "We call 'em slushies."

Uncle Dale and I traded looks. What do you say to a living snowman?

"You know, you really shouldn't smoke," I blurted.

General Frostman smirked. "Right, and those powder punks shouldn't be tryin' to freeze my butt off."

We climbed out of the crevasse. Uncle Dale grabbed

General Frostman's hand. "General J. R. Frostman Jr.! What an honor. I've heard so much about you."

"Is that a flame thrower?" I interrupted.

"No!" General Frostman said. "This here's my angel duster."

Phil and Gumdrop ran up. The general glared at them. "What are humans doing past the barrier?"

"Humblest apologies, General Frostman!" Phil said. "They're with us. We've come to see the big man."

Frostman turned to me. "She's the one?" he asked.

Phil nodded.

The general slowly shook his head, turned, and started wobbling away. "We're doomed."

Chapter Seventeen

"Pay the general no heed," said Gumdrop. "He can be a little cranky."

Slowly, the blizzard passed over. Eventually I

could see past my nose to the endless frozen wasteland around us. Which begged the question:

"You told me you burned that!" cried Gumdrop.

Phil smiled. "I lied."

I said, "What did the general mean when he asked if I was the one?"

"He knows you're here for the appeal," said Phil.

"How come he got the message and no one else did?" I asked.

Phil and Gumdrop shared another look.

"The cell reception up here is quite spotty," said Gumdrop.

Phil pointed to his phone. "See, no bars!"

"But don't you and Uncle Dale text?" I asked.

The general interrupted. "We're here."

I said, "We're where?"

And then I saw it. The North Pole. Or Cleveland. I wasn't sure.

"That's it?" I asked.

"That's it," said Phil.

No way. The North Pole is supposed to be this happy place full of whimsy and good tidings. The snow is coconut frosting (and NEVER yellow). The elves make merry while they build toys with their tiny hands (using tiny power tools). Reindeer play reindeer games like checkers and Texas Hold'em. And Santa is right in the middle of it all telling hilarious elf jokes. . . .

It's true! It's in all the snow globes!

But what was in front of me was not snow globe friendly.

Gumdrop sensed I was disappointed. "Yes, she was once a great and magical city. But things have changed. Let's not fret about that now. First, we've got a little boy to get off the Naughty List."

"And to do that," said Phil, "we've got to get you to the man."

"Santa?" I asked.

Phil nodded to the general. The general turned and blasted a hole in the ice with his angel duster/hair dryer. Then he started barking like a . . .

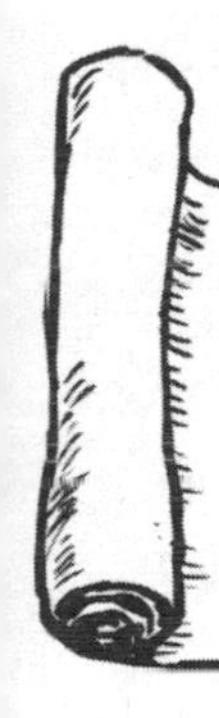

Chapter Eighteen

There are six seals in Seal Team Nine. Actually there are five seals and Blutarski.

I looked at Uncle Dale. "Seriously?"

"I'm sure they're quite professional," said Uncle Dale just before Blutarski tried to balance the team leader on his nose.

"Put me down, Blutarski!" screamed the team leader. "Stick to the mission. Step one: wrap the package!"

Blutarski slowly nodded. "Oh, right."

Blutarski threw dark clothes at Uncle Dale and me. "Put these on."

I inspected the clothes. "You want us all in black?"

"This time of year it's dark twenty-three hours a day and going ninja will disguise you from the Watcher," said Phil.

Blutarski saluted the team leader. "The packages are wrapped, sir. Permission to transport."

"Permission granted," said the team leader. "Operation Drone Drop is under way."

That's when it became clear exactly how they were going to get us to Santa.

Uncle Dale, Gumdrop, Phil, and I were each buckled to a harness around a seal. As the ground dropped away, General Frostman and his troops saluted.

General Frostman growled at us, "Don't screw this up."

I turned to Uncle Dale. "What's he talking about?"

"Quiet," commanded the team leader. "Silence the rest of the way."

Uncle Dale shrugged. I couldn't help feeling like this was an awful lot of effort to get one little boy off the Naughty List.

Below us lay the smoke-belching workshops of the North Pole.

After a minute or so I spotted something odd in the distance. At first it looked like a dense forest of short, leafy green shrubs. But when we got closer I realized they weren't shrubs. They were . . . are you kidding me? . . . FEET? Seriously, it looked like half-buried feet sticking out of the ground.

And in the center of the fleshy forest was a thick, brown swamp that belched and moaned like a gassy volcano.

"What's that?" I whisper-shouted.

"That, my good friend, is the Figgy Pudding Swamp surrounded by the Missile-Toe grove," replied Gumdrop.

As we flew closer we also climbed higher.

"Why are we going up?" I asked.

"INCOMING!" yelled the platoon leader.

"A Yule log!" cried Phil. "If you get too close the missile toes will fire."

"And if you get shot down into the figgy pudding," added Gumdrop, "you're deader than a Christmas ham!"

"Seriously? Figgy pudding?" I pleaded.

"It's like quicksand, only more delicious. It sucks you under slowly . . . the harder you flail, the quicker you sink," said Phil.

There's a point where so many things get so weird that they're no longer weird, they're normal.

Is that still weird?

Whatever. We cleared the Figgy Pudding Swamp and its toe defenders. The Seal Team dropped us on higher ground near a clearing.

Phil pointed down a narrow path. "This way. We've got to hurry. We've only got two and a half days until Christmas."

Wait. I was confused.

Again.

"That doesn't make sense," I said. "It was seven thirty on Christmas Eve when we left."

"We're on Trans-Dimensional time now," said Gumdrop. "An hour of human time is like a day of our time."

"So time moves . . . what? Slower here?"

"From a human perspective: faster," said Gumdrop.

"From our perspective: slower. How do you think we make toys for every kid on earth and deliver them in one night?" added Phil.

"Magic?" I said.

"Simple quantum physics," said Uncle Dale. "We're in a parallel alternate dimension operating on a different clock speed."

Gumdrop said, "Like we explained, magic has its limitations.

"And, of course, there's the smell," added Gumdrop.

"Refried beans." Phil nodded.

Wait. He was right. That was the smell back in Tad's room.

"We're here," said Phil.

In front of us stood a ratty, beat-up trailer.

Uncle Dale pointed. "Is the big man inside?"

Phil and Gumdrop nodded.

"Santa?" I asked. "Already? Don't I get to, like, take a shower or watch some sort of instructional 'How to Save Your Brother's Christmas' video?"

"Relax," said Phil. "You're going to do great."

He eyed me with doughy, sleep-filled eyes. He blinked twice and just for a moment, there was a spark of recognition. Then nothing.

Just a fat man.

Scratching his butt.

Chapter Nineteen

Santa's trailer had seen better days.

Actually, Santa had seen better days.

We all know he's a bit on the husky side. (It's hard to exercise in such a cold climate.) But nobody warned me about his general lack of hygiene (a big word my mom likes to use when she's trying to get Tad to take a bath).

Phil cleared his throat.

Santa didn't look up from his tablet. "What part of 'get off my lawn' don't you understand?"

Gumdrop stepped forward: "I, Gumdrop Q. Schmelzer, being of sound mind and body, do attempt to bring forth a case in front of the honorable Judge Kristopher Kringle AKA Santa Claus, per article 24 C, subsection D of the North Pole Regional Circuit Court of Appeals that hereby states—"

Santa glared at us. "You've got to be kidding."

Phil continued, "Sir, we're appealing a young child's placement on the Naughty List."

Santa snorted. "You're not kidding."

"I would like the court to acknowledge Bobbie Rose Mendoza and her legal representation Dale Andrew Mendoza," said Gumdrop.

I flashed my brightest Hey-Santa-I've-come-a-long-way-and-was-almost-killed-by-whales/candy canes/snow angels-so-it'd-be-really-nice-if-you-just-took-my-brother-off-this-stupid-Naughty-List-so-I-can-go-home smile.

Gumdrop turned to Uncle Dale. "Your turn."

Uncle Dale was shaking like a cat getting a bath. "I . . . I can't."

I stared at him. "What do you mean you can't?"

"I just . . . can't," he said.

"But I can't do it," I told him. "He doesn't want to hear from me."

Uncle Dale backed toward the door. "You can do it, Bobbie. You can do anything," he said as he fled the trailer.

I looked at Santa. He yawned.

"FINE!" I said. "Santa, so hey, it's me, Bobbie. You probably don't know who I am, but whatever . . . Look, my little brother, Tad, loves you and that whole Christmas thing you do. So yeah, he got in big trouble for something really stupid that I did, so I'd really appreciate it if you'd just do me a solid and—"

"Hey! HEY!!!" I yelled. "I came a long way!"

Santa startled awake. "You're still here? Look, kid, whatever you want, I can't give it to you."

He plugged in his earbuds and went back to staring at his tablet. Gumdrop grabbed me by my shoulder and steered me toward the door. But I wasn't ready to go.

I grabbed Santa's tablet out of his hands and threw it to the floor. "Look at you! You're pathetic! You have the power to help save my brother's Christmas and all you can do is sit there like a fat slob! I was never sure you were real, but I still believed in you. But now that

I know you're real . . . I DON'T BELIEVE IN YOU AT ALL!"

Santa stared at me. Once again, for a brief moment there was that twinkle of recognition. He saw me, all of me, who I was, who I am, and who I could be.

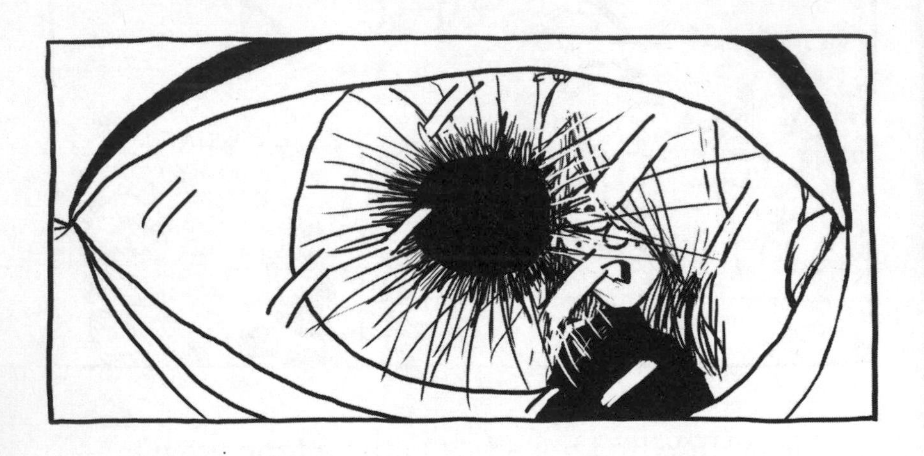

Then he belched.

Chapter Twenty

The four of us stood outside the trailer. I wanted to scream until my lungs hurt. Not only was Santa a total jerk, but Uncle Dale—who never met a stranger he didn't want to debate Bigfoot's shoe size with—TOTALLY CLAMMED UP!

"You tried," said Gumdrop.

I glared at him. "I failed."

"Bobbie, I'm so sorry," said Uncle Dale. "It's just . . . I thought he . . . I couldn't."

"You thought he . . . ?" I closed my eyes. "I don't

care. Can we please just go home now?"

"Pssst," said a voice behind us.

We turned around. A reindeer was peering out from the side of the trailer. An actual reindeer. With antlers and everything! But there was something strange about him. I mean, other than the fact that he talked. It took me a second, but then I saw it: the tips of his antlers glowed bright red.

"It's okay," said Phil. "Larry's with us."

Larry? Wait. There's Donner and Dasher and Comet and . . . whatever. I never heard of Larry.

We followed him around the trailer, down an icy path that lead straight to . . .

Larry picked his way through broken bits of wood and plastic, around a huge twisted ball of wire, over a pile of crushed circuit boards, then stopped in front of a central mound of mostly intact garbage bags.

Gumdrop reached into the mound and yanked. A bag-covered door swung open, revealing steps leading down into the dark. "After you," he said.

"You're kidding," I said.

"It's perfectly safe," said Gumdrop.

"Except when it isn't," added Phil.

"Someone's coming! Hurry!" hissed Larry.

We clamored down the steps while Uncle Dale slammed the door shut behind us. The only light was the glow from Larry's antlers.

The steps led down about thirty feet and stopped in front of a metal door. Larry knocked with his antlers. A voice inside said, "Jingle Bells."

Larry answered, "Batman smells."

"Because all he eats . . . ," called the voice.

"Is refried beans," said Larry.

What is it with this place and refried beans?

The door swung open to reveal another reindeer. This one was stocky and looked like he worked out. Past him was a large room filled with more reindeer. Some were working out on gym equipment. Others were playing a video game. And a separate group was playing poker.

"Poker?" I asked.

Larry piped up, "Would you rather play Twister? I love Twister! Please, let's play Twister!"

"No Twister!" cried all the reindeer at once.

"I'll pass," I said. "What I really want is to go home." I stared at Larry's glowing antlers. "What is the deal with your . . ."

Larry looked up. His antlers were glowing brighter and brighter. "Oh my! That is unexpected. This only happens—"

"Never mind the freak," said a voice from the poker table. "I'm Dancer, and this is Dasher, Prancer, and Donner. That's Vixen and Blitzen working out. And the gamers are Comet and Cupid."

They all stopped what they were doing and stared at me.

"She's the one?" asked Comet.

"According to the freak's antlers," said Dancer.

I turned to Larry. His antlers were almost on fire.

"The cheer is strong in this one," said Vixen.

The what?

Dancer looked at Phil and Gumdrop. "Did it work?"

The two elves slowly shook their heads. The reindeer all groaned.

"Did what work?" I asked.

"Well, it was worth a shot," said Prancer.

Dancer looked at me. "Thanks for the effort, kid. Have a safe trip home."

"Whoa-whoa-whoa!" I cried. "Cheer? Did what work? Wait. No. First . . ."

Blixen chuckled. "She's never heard of Larry, the red-antlered reindeer."

Donner smiled. "But I bet she's heard of—"

"Yeah. The other one," I said.

"He's a myth," said Dancer. "A PR stunt to drum up cheer."

Larry protested, "It's not a complete myth. There was a storm. I did light the way."

"When you weren't colliding with commercial aircraft," said Cupid.

"One jet!" said Larry. "And we didn't collide. It was a near miss."

"When you lost control of your bladder it wasn't a near miss," said Dancer.

"I apologized for that. And besides I wear a . . . a protective absorbent garment now," said Larry.

"A diaper," said Comet.

"Enough!" I yelled. "Too much information! Next question: I wasn't brought up here to just get Tad off the Naughty List, was I?"

Everyone went quiet. Phil and Gumdrop shared a look. Then Phil said, "We brought you up here to save Christmas. We thought if you appealed to Santa it would shake something loose."

"Why in the world would you think I could help?" I asked.

"Because you're special."

"I'm not special. I keep trying to tell everyone, but no one listens."

"That's not true, Bobbie," said Uncle Dale.

"How would you know? Nothing you do matters either!" I cried.

As the words flew out of my mouth and I saw Uncle Dale's face, I wished with all my heart I could grab them and shove them back down my throat.

But I couldn't.

"None of it matters anymore," said Phil. "It's all over. Christmas is doomed."

"Doomed?" I said.

WHAM! WHAM

The entire room shook. Someone or something was trying to get through the door.

"OH NO!" shouted Phil. "He's found us!"

"He must have sensed the increased cheer levels!" said Gumdrop.

"Who found us?" I asked.

"The Abdominal Snowman!" shouted Gumdrop.

"The Watcher's Snow Henchman!" Phil cried.

I said, "You mean the Abominable Snow—"

He was a snow-hulk on steroids! He was about to kick butt and take names—MY NAME!

Vixen went at him with a flying head butt and ended up splattered against his snow-abs like a bird hitting a window.

"BRING ME THE HUMAN!" he bellowed.

Dancer grabbed me and shoved me behind a wall of reindeer and elves.

"What human?" said Phil.

The snow-zilla grabbed Phil by the neck and yanked him off his feet. "Tell me, missile-toe bait!"

I raised my hand. "I'm right here!"

I pushed past Dancer. "You want me? Leave them alone."

The snow-hulk started to reach for me, but not before . . .

Did Ninja Santa just save the day? There's no way that could be that same slob of a Santa I saw earlier.

But it was the same Santa. Same gut. Same itchy butt. Same crazy beard. But this time with an actual twinkle in his eye. Oh yeah, and he put on deodorant—Cinnamon Sport, I think.

As the snow-hulk moaned, the reindeer quickly tied him up.

Larry's antlers erupted in bright flames. Santa looked at me. "Whoa. The cheer is strong in this one."

"Me?" I said.

Santa smiled. "We're going to need all you can muster."

"We?" I asked.

"Yes, Bobbie," said Santa as he gestured to the group. "We're going to destroy the Watcher."

Chapter Twenty-One

We're going to destroy the Watcher? We? I've always had a problem with we. Me, I can rely on. We? Not so much.

I came to the North Pole to get my brother off the Naughty List. Simple. Straightforward. We? Not so simple. Not so straightforward.

It was time for some answers. "I'm not here to get my brother off the Naughty List, am I?" I asked again.

"Yes. And no," said Santa. "Mostly no."

I looked at Phil and Gumdrop. "You lied to me."

"No," said Gumdrop. "We told you the truth."

"Just not all of the truth," said Phil.

"We were parceling it out to you in tiny little bits," said Gumdrop.

"Kinda like a pie . . . you can't eat an entire pie in just one sitting. You gotta go piece by piece," added Phil.

"What Phil and Gumdrop are trying to say," said Santa, "is that Tad will get off the Naughty List when you help us destroy the Watcher."

I shook my head. "Give me one good reason why I should help."

Silence. Then . . . "You're the only one who can," said Santa.

"Me?" I asked. "You're Santa Claus! You've got elves! And snowmen with semi-automatic hair dryers! And reindeer with freaky glowing antlers. And magic! Serious magic!"

Santa smiled. "Magic has its limitations."

I rolled my eyes. "Is that, like, printed on your business card?"

"We need cheer," said Santa. "And you've got it."

Larry pointed to his glowing antlers. "Crazy cheer."

Phil nodded. "The most cheer."

"Well, now, technically not the most cheer," said Gumdrop.

"Not helping!" said Phil.

"We need to be straight with her," said Gumdrop. "There are four others with superior cheer, but they're . . . well . . . they're not available."

"You're special, Bobbie," said Santa. "You can make a difference!"

I looked to Uncle Dale. He smiled and nodded. "You can, Bobbie. You really can."

Wait. No. It doesn't make sense.

"I was ignoring Christmas! Christmas bullied me! I tackled it off a roof!" I showed Santa my arm. "Christmas broke my arm!"

Santa smiled. "Cheer isn't simply blind enthusiasm, Bobbie. Real cheer comes from not accepting any substitute for the real thing. You knew Christmas without your dad wouldn't be Christmas."

Phil added, "Trying to win Tad's present at the toy store sent your cheer levels through the roof."

"I don't understand," I said. "Why does the Watcher have to be destroyed? I thought you created the Watcher to increase the amount of cheer."

"It did increase it," said Santa. "At first."

"Yes!" said Santa. "If we don't stop the Watcher tonight, Christmas will be canceled!"

All the elves and reindeer nodded.

"So that's why I'm here?" I asked.

Santa nodded. "That's why you're here."

"But how can *I* help?"

"You already have," said Santa. "What you said back in the trailer. It woke me up. It's all that cheer. It's . . . you know . . . contagious."

"You're saying I'm a disease?" I said. "Great."

"No! Not at all," said Santa. "Here, sit down. I need to tell you something very important."

"We both love waffle-pops," said Santa. "We both have a love/hate thing going on with Christmas."

"You too?" I asked.

"I have a confession to make, Bobbie," whispered Santa as he leaned in to my ear. "Don't tell anybody, but sometimes I doubt whether or not Christmas is worth it."

"Dude, that's messed up!" I said.

"I know," said Santa. "All the hard work, the stress, the intense elf labor. Did you know I'm afraid of heights? What I'm trying to say is . . . sometimes the greatest things in life are the things you question . . . things you sometimes dislike. I lost sight of that, but you and your cheer helped me get it back."

Wow . . . Santa's got issues. But I guess I do too. Plus he digs waffle-pops so . . . you know . . . there's that.

"Tell me, Bobbie, what do you want for Christmas?" Santa asked.

"That's easy," I said. "I want what Tad asked for in his letter. I want my dad to come home from North Dakota so we can be a family again."

"I want to give you that, Bobbie. I really do. But I can't do it without Christmas. And I can't save Christmas without you."

I took out the locket Mom gave me and opened it. I stared at my reflection. "I . . . I matter."

Santa smiled. "Of course you do."

Chapter Twenty-Two

"Where is this kill switch?" I asked.

"The last place anyone would look, including the Watcher," said Santa. "I hid it with . . ."

"What did he do?" I asked.

"What *didn't* he do? You know, some kids are just mean," said Santa.

Yeah, I knew.

"So all we gotta do is find the kill switch, push a button, and Christmas is saved?"

"Unfortunately it's not that easy. The switch must be plugged into the Watcher directly."

"Ah, c'mon! Haven't you guys ever heard of Bluetooth or Wi-Fi!" I said.

"Forget that," said Santa. "Before we can even get to the switch we have to get my sleigh. And to do that we need a plan."

I'm pretty good at planning stuff. Like when Dad used to put up Christmas decorations.

CHRISTMAS PREP TO-DO LIST

- [x] 1. WAKE UP DAD SUPER EARLY.
- [x] 2. EAT FOUR WAFFLE-POPS.
- [x] 3. GET LIGHTS AND TREE FROM SCARY ATTIC.
- [x] 4. HANG LIGHTS ON ROOF.
- [x] ~~5. DON'T FALL OFF ROOF~~
- [x] 6. ONLY FALL OFF ROOF ONCE.

So when Santa ran through his big master to-do list I kept thorough notes.

SANTA'S PLAN TO SAVE CHRISTMAS

- [ ] 1. BREAK INTO WORKSHOP.
- [ ] 2. FREE THE SLEIGH.
- [ ] 3. RETRIEVE KILL SWITCH.
- [ ] 4. RETURN TO NORTH POLE.
- [ ] 5. DISABLE WATCHER.
- [ ] 6. CELEBRATE WITH EPICALLY AWESOME ELF DANCE PARTY.

Easy-peasy, right?

Wrong.

Larry raised a hoof. "Even if we can get in the workshop and past the guards, the sleigh is completely frozen in a massive block of ice."

Santa chuckled. "If only there was a way to generate a massive amount of concentrated heat—like a flame. A flame hot enough to melt a massive block of ice in minutes."

All the other reindeer rolled their reindeer eyes as Larry cracked the tiniest of reindeer smiles.

Santa let loose a hearty belly laugh. "Larry . . . won't you fry my sleigh tonight?"

Chapter Twenty-Three

Before we set out for the workshop, everyone got their ninja suits on so the Watcher would be blind to our presence.

I caught Uncle Dale just before he put his ninja mask on.

"It's nice to feel invisible sometimes," he said.

"Uncle Dale . . . are you okay?" I asked. "You seem different."

"Just bad memories, kid . . . ," he said.

"What do you mean? What happened? You've been here before, haven't you?" I asked.

"Old news, kid. A story for another time," he said in a way that made it clear he didn't want to talk about it.

"I'm sorry about what I said earlier."

"You were right, though. I'm forty years old and I live in my brother's basement."

"I know I call you crazy and weird and I tease you sometimes . . . but I'm really glad you've been living with us. This year would have been way lamer without you."

Uncle Dale smiled for a brief moment, then pulled his ninja mask down over his face. "Ditto, kiddo."

We left the dump and carefully worked our way to a hill overlooking Santa's workshop—or what was left of it.

"Your sleigh is in there?" I cried.

"There must be a hundred EWAs guarding it," said Phil.

Gumdrop said, "That's a hundred versus . . ."

"Once again we're doomed," said Phil.

"No, we're not," said Uncle Dale. "We just need a diversion. A naughty diversion."

We all stared at Uncle Dale. That crazy look in his eye was back.

"Huh?" I asked as Uncle Dale started taking off his ninja suit.

"Stop!" said Gumdrop. "If you take that off the—"

"The Watcher will see him being naughty," explained Santa.

"Yes! And divert the EWAs away from the workshop," said Phil.

"Can elves and reindeer get put on the Naughty List?" I asked.

Phil laughed. "We helped build it . . . of course we can."

And with that, Phil, Gumdrop, Uncle Dale, and the reindeer went from all ninja to all naughty. . . .

Santa, Larry, and I watched the guards immediately turn in the direction of the Naughty-fest.

"It's working!" I cried.

Santa grabbed Larry and me. "You two follow me."

We slipped off to the side while the guards abandoned their posts to chase the Naughty Eleven. When the coast was clear, we entered the workshop.

"Stay down and keep a lookout," said Santa. "There are still EWAs inside."

We tiptoed quietly past the assembly line and the abandoned Reindeer Rec Room until we finally found the sleigh garage, or as Santa liked to call it . . .

"Light it up, Larry!" said Santa.

I noticed a blue light coming from farther into the workshop. I don't know why I decided I needed to check it out. It's like that time I was absolutely convinced the dog would look better if I painted his ears and tail purple using crayons I melted in the microwave.

I'm a kid. Stuff happens.

As Santa and Larry went to work de-icing the sleigh, I headed toward the blue light.

IT WAS COMING FROM A CLOSED DOOR.
AUTHORIZED PERSONNEL ONLY

I TIPTOED UP AS QUIETLY AS I COULD.

AND SLOWLY, SUPER SLOWLY I OPENED THE DOOR TO...

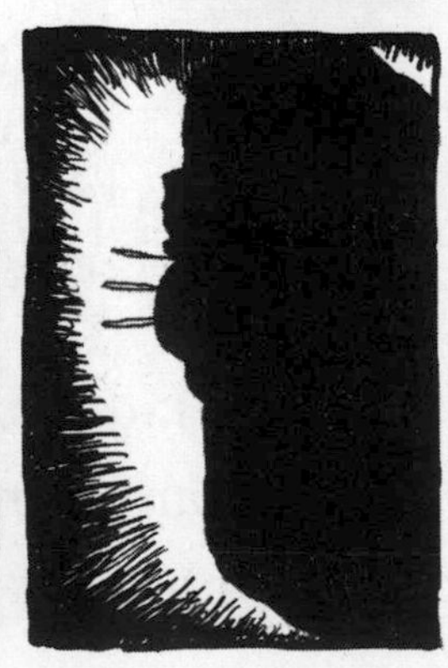

. . . beyond creepy. The Watcher was made of parts

of old toys. It had an old doll's head, arms made of hobbyhorses, and a hockey-sticks-and-skateboard body. All poking out of a jack-in-the-box.

After a few seconds I took another peek. The Watcher had turned back to the monitors. Right in front was a computer monitor. It gave me an idea. Why can't I just search for Tad's name and delete it? Or delete all the names? I stared at the screen and remembered the time I was nine and accidentally deleted an entire hard drive trying to Photoshop a booger out of my nose in a selfie. If I could do it once by accident, I could certainly do it once on purpose.

While the Watcher's eye was still focused on the monitors, I quietly approached the terminal and typed in "Mendoza."

Uncle Dale? Why is Uncle Dale listed as naughty?

Before I could find the delete button, I heard a high-pitched whine. I looked up . . .

The Watcher's eye was moving toward me. I had to hide. But where?

"Bobbie!" whispered Santa behind me.

I turned to see Santa at the door. He whispered, "Get behind me! NOW!"

I dove behind Santa just before the eye had me in its sights.

We backed out of the room then sprinted toward the freshly thawed sleigh.

Santa barred the door behind us. “Hop in, kid!”

I jumped in the still-damp backseat as Santa and Larry pushed the sleigh out of the Elf Cave doors. About fifty yards away was the takeoff platform at the top of what looked like the world’s largest ski jump.

“We’re going down that?” I cried.

"It takes a bit of speed to get this flying brick into the air," said Santa. "With or without eight reindeer."

"Wait," I said. "What do you mean 'without eight reindeer'?"

"With Larry and your cheer we might be able to fly alone," said Santa.

"Might?" said Larry and me at the same time.

WOO-HO WOO-HO

"Attention all Elfbots, arrest Christmas Enemy Number One!" yelled a scary robot voice as EWAs pounded at the barred door behind us.

"We've got to go now!" Larry exclaimed.

"No!" I yelled. "I can't!"

Santa started to push the sleigh down the ramp. "You can, Bobbie!"

I screamed, "No, really! I—"

Uncle Dale ran up with Phil, Gumdrop, and the other reindeer in tow.

"What took so long?" asked Santa.

Uncle Dale eyed Phil. "Some of us enjoyed being naughty a bit more than others."

"I can't help it if I have wicked strong wedgie skills," said Phil.

"Forget it!" yelled Santa. "Get yourselves harnessed so we can blow this pop stand!"

Who talks like that?

"They're almost through the door," I yelled.

"They're after me!" said Santa. "I'll distract them. The rest of you retrieve the kill switch."

Uncle Dale looked Santa up and down. "What size are you? A fifty-two wide?"

"What?" asked Santa.

"It's a bit big for me, but I'll make it work. Now lose that ninja gear and the Santa suit underneath," said Uncle Dale as he started to strip.

"No. You can't," said Santa.

Uncle Dale shook his head. "I can . . ."

Chapter Twenty-Four

You wouldn't think Uncle Dale could fit into Santa's suit, but being a 24/7 semiprofessional internet crank living in a dark basement tends to do damage to your waistline.

A couple dozen extra belt cinches and Santa's suit fit just fine.

Suddenly Santa stopped and stared at Dale. Maybe it was the sight of him in the Santa suit, or maybe it was the fact that he'd removed the spaghetti strainer from his head. But Santa seemed to recognize him. "Wait a minute . . . I know you."

"You remember?" Dale asked.

"Of course I remember . . . you were the bravest kid I ever met."

"Uncle Dale?" I said. But before I could find out more, Santa tugged at his beard and detached a long tuft of curly white hair and handed it to Uncle Dale.

"You're really going to need this," said Santa.

Uncle Dale put on the beard as the reindeer finished attaching themselves to the sleigh.

I hopped in next to Santa, Phil, and Gumdrop as Uncle Dale moved around to the back of the sleigh.

The EWAs had breached the door!

"Y'all need to get out of here. NOW!" yelled Uncle Dale as he gave the sleigh a shove.

We slid toward the ramp. Behind us Uncle Dale channeled his inner elf.

It worked! The EWAs went after Uncle Dale like a stupid robot dog after a stupid robot bone. Or something.

Meanwhile nine reindeer who hadn't flown together in years were having more than a little trouble getting their act together.

Suddenly, a rogue EWA—who I guess didn't fall for Uncle Dale's ruse—appeared out of nowhere and leaped onto Larry's back.

"He's trying to cut the reins!" I cried.

"Phil! Gumdrop!" Santa shouted.

The two elves were already a step ahead as they each reached under the seat of the sleigh and grabbed two Christmas cannons.

The EWA dodged the terrifying tangled-light barrage like he'd seen it all before. Phil and Gumdrop kept firing, but the robot elf was too fast for them.

Meanwhile, Larry, distracted by the EWA on his back, wasn't paying attention.

Phil turned to Gumdrop. “It’s time.”

Gumdrop yelled, “No! Absolutely not!”

“But you’re so good at it!” said Phil.

“It’s demeaning!”

Phil grabbed Gumdrop, reared back, and . . .

Direct hit. Gumdrop collided with the EWA, causing them both to tumble toward the ground and out of sight.

“Where’s Gumdrop? Where’d he go?” yelled Phil.

"HELP!" screamed a tiny elf voice.

I looked down to see Gumdrop being dragged through the snow by the sleigh; his coat was snagged on one of the wooden skids.

Phil leaned over the back of the sleigh and screamed. "I'll save you, buddy!"

"Look out! We're headed over the cliff!" yelled Santa. "I need some help here!"

While Phil dropped down to help Gumdrop, I grabbed the reins with Santa.

"To the right!" yelled Santa. "Steer Larry right!"

We both yanked hard on the reins as Phil grabbed Gumdrop's waistband.

We careened back onto the takeoff path, hitting a large buried chunk of ice in the process.

KA-CHUNK!

Phil lost his grip. He and Gumdrop (minus his pants) disappeared in the snow.

Just as we were about to clear the edge of the jump I looked back.

Suddenly my stomach was in my mouth. I turned around. Bad idea.

A lot of people might call it adrenaline; I just call it "Oh no, I don't want to die in a horrific reindeer crash at the bottom of a North Pole Slip 'N Slide."

"We don't have enough speed!" Santa yelled.

That's when I gripped the reins tighter and shouted at the top of my lungs.

Nothing. I turned to Santa. He pointed. "You forgot one."

I screamed, "ON LARRY!"

I had to duck as Larry's antlers exploded into a fiery ball that somehow rocketed us all off the end of the ramp and into the sky.

I looked back toward the North Pole . . . wondering if I'd ever see it again.

That's when I noticed a familiar, refried beans–ish smell.

Then everything turned red, then green, then . . .

. . . black.

Chapter Twenty-Five

I don't know if you've ever jumped dimensions in a reindeer-propelled sleigh, but it does a real number on your hair.

Luckily Santa had Uncle Dale's spaghetti strainer on his head, and he's pretty much bald, but what was left of his beard didn't hold up too well.

I managed to tame my hair before we gently landed on a frozen rooftop in the middle of a snowy suburb. It sort of looked like my neighborhood (though Santa assured me it wasn't).

I pulled out the rap sheet on Craig Bipple. Let's just say his reputation as the Naughtiest Child in the World was well earned.

And those were just the domestic offenses. He had pages and pages of naughty stuff both at school and away from home. This kid was just mean. Some kids are, you know.

"The Kill Switch is hidden somewhere in his room," said Santa as he climbed out of the sleigh and approached Craig's window. "You keep a lookout and make sure the kid doesn't wake up while I find it."

"Wait a sec," I interrupted. "What about the chimney?"

"It is a nice chimney," observed Santa.

I said, "No. Don't you slide down the chimney?"

"Not with my asthma. Windows are much better. Front doors are ideal. I also prefer oatmeal raisin to chocolate chip, and I don't drink milk because I'm somewhat lactose intolerant."

Santa quietly opened the window and slipped inside.

Something didn't feel right. For starters, the kid sure didn't look that naughty. His room was neat and tidy. It didn't smell like gross socks or moldy toenails. It looked like the normal room of an average kid.

Even the pictures on his dresser seemed normal.

"Found it," Santa whispered as he pulled what looked like an old remote control out from inside a toy robot.

I inspected the photo.

Craig grabbed a rope from under his bed and before I could blink, Santa was hanging upside down and tied up in the middle of the room.

Santa tossed me the Kill Switch. “Go! Go! Go!”

But I didn’t go. I froze.

“Bobbie! You can do this,” cried Santa. “I know you can!”

Before I could think, porch lights started popping on up and down the block.

Larry waved me toward the sleigh. “C’mon! We have to go! We can’t get caught up here!”

I was scared. I couldn’t move. . . .

“NOW!” yelled Larry.

I heard a door open below. I turned to look. When I turned back the sleigh was gone.

Now I was alone.

Completely alone. And as I looked through the window into Craig Bipple’s room, I was reminded of a familiar sight. I looked down at the Kill Switch and then to Santa.

Uncle Dale, Mom, Santa . . . they were right. What I did mattered. But where they were wrong was thinking that I could make things better. Especially when it was totally obvious . . .

I looked at Santa and shook my head. "I'm sorry . . . I can't!"

I dropped the Kill Switch, hopped off the roof, and took off running.

Chapter Twenty-Six

I was cold. I was running. Why was I running? I don't like running.

But it was the only thing I could do. I couldn't stay. I couldn't help. But I could run. I could be invisible. Because in the end: I really don't matter.

When I try to matter I break my arm and then accidentally become a thief and then ruin my brother's Christmas and then get my uncle captured by robot elves and then get Santa kidnapped by the naughtiest kid in the world.

So yeah, I'm running. If there was a way I could run away from myself I would.

After five minutes I realized I had a problem: I didn't know where I was.

That's when a pair of headlights hit me from down the road. Who is it this time?

No, there were no trans-dimensional busybodies this time. Just a police car. Couldn't they see I was invisible?

"LEAVE ME ALONE!" I shouted.

"Mandan PD . . . Young lady, are you all right?" shouted a woman's voice from the car.

I just stared at her. How could I even begin to explain?

When she stepped into the glow of the headlights I was able to make out her face. She was young—maybe late twenties. Her long blonde hair was twisted up in a bun. She didn't look like a cop.

The cop continued, "My name's Andrea. Friends call me Andy. What's yours?"

"Roberta," I said. "But everyone calls me Bobbie."

"What's going on, Bobbie?"

"It's a long, weird story. . . ."

She smiled at me. And not an Oh-you-stupid-kid smile, but an actual I-think-I-get-it smile.

"Copy that. Christmas can be a bummer sometimes. But here's the problem . . . It's eleven degrees out right now. And it's about an hour before midnight when my shift ends."

"So?" I asked.

"Welp, how 'bout this . . . Why don't I give you a lift to the station? We've got hot chocolate with an unlimited supply of marshmallows. You can call your folks. I'm sure they're worried."

"Wait a minute . . . what police department did you say you worked for?" I asked.

"Mandan. Mandan, North Dakota."

"North Dakota? My dad lives in North Dakota!"

"Whereabouts?"

"Bismark."

"Okay, then; that's about a twenty-minute drive . . . fifteen if I use my siren."

I didn't say anything. Not because I didn't want to see my dad, but because I didn't know what I would say to him if I did . . . especially about what exactly I was doing here.

Andy kneeled down next to me. "Look, Bobbie, Christmas and I used to have issues too. Always made me miss my mom. But running away isn't the answer. So how about you hop in my old sleigh here and we burn rubber to your dad's place and get you in bed before Santa comes. How's that sound?"

Chapter Twenty-Seven

Turns out, Dad wasn't as mad as I thought he would be. Or as he could be.

He asked me all the normal questions. "What are you doing here? Did you run away? Did you hitchhike? Oh please God, tell me you didn't hitchhike!" I gave him zero answers.

He tried calling Mom a few times but got no answer.

"She must already be asleep . . . ," he said. "No need to worry her this late, especially since you're all right."

But he knew I wasn't "all right." And he knew if he pushed me I wasn't going to talk. There was only one way I'd voluntarily open up.

"I'll heat you up some if you talk to me," he added.

I keep forgetting: like Mom, he's a Jedi-parent too.

I was about six bites into Dad's world-famous meat cake when I noticed . . .

"But it's just you," I said.

Dad grinned. "Rub it in, why don't ya?"

"But why decorate when we're not here?"

"That's exactly why I do it. It makes me think of you guys. All of this reminds me of your mom and you and your brother . . . and my brother too."

I glanced over at a picture of Dad and Uncle Dale as kids on the wall.

"You know . . . it's funny," said Dad. "Uncle Dale ran away on Christmas Eve once too. I think he was about your age."

Wait a minute . . . Uncle Dale was on the Naughty List. I saw it in the Watcher's lair. Also, Santa seemed to know him.

Was this running away on Christmas thing the reason he was on the Naughty List?

"What happened?" I asked.

Dad frowned. "No one knows. But I'll never forget that night. Everyone in town was looking for him. It was dark and below freezing and we had no idea where he was."

"What . . . Where'd he go?!" I asked.

"He'd been gone for about six or seven hours when he showed up . . . just after midnight."

"Where?"

"In his closet. I guess he'd been in there all along, although I could have sworn I'd already looked."

"Did he say where he went?" I asked.

"Kind of. Not really. No one could really make much sense of it. But the strangest part was that he was covered in melted snow and tinsel and leaves. He looked frozen, like he'd been off in the woods for days. He smelled terrible, too. Like . . ."

"How did you know?" asked Dad.

"Lucky guess."

Dad continued, "Uncle Dale was different after that. He kept talking about Santa and the elves and some machine . . . something happened to him that night. No one really knows."

But I knew. Uncle Dale had been to the North Pole before. But why? Had he tried to stop the Watcher too, a long time ago?

"For some reason after that night he never thought much of himself," Dad explained. "It's like he faded away. Like he thought that nothing he did could ever make a difference. Like nothing he did mattered."

But I knew Uncle Dale had made a difference! He sacrificed himself so that Santa and I could make it across the Trans-Dimensional Barrier . . . so I could get the Kill Switch . . . so . . .

. . . I COULD SAVE CHRISTMAS!

What had I done! How could I have been so stupid?

"No time for what?" asked Dad.

I stared at my meat cake. "Nothing."

Dad sighed. "What do you say we get some sleep before Santa gets here? You can tell me everything in the morning when we get your mom on the phone."

I didn't know what to do. Here it was about to be midnight; I had no Kill Switch and no way of getting to the North Pole!

That's when I noticed something strange. Out Dad's front window, past the parking lot of the apartment complex, past the small tree-lined highway . . . was a bright, flickering light, getting closer. And closer.

And closer.

Dad noticed it too. "What in the world is that?"

Nine reindeer and an empty sleigh lay in a jumble in my dad's living room. Eight reindeer all yelled at once, "LARRY!"

"Taking off without the big guy is easy," said Larry. "Landing? Not so much."

"Dad! Are you okay?" I cried.

Dasher checked my dad's pulse with his hoof. "He's fine. . . . Just a bad bump on the noggin."

"What are you doing here?" I said. "You left without me!"

Comet said, "We couldn't risk being spotted so we took off into a holding pattern until things calmed down."

"By the time we got back you were long gone," added Cupid.

"Where's Santa?" I asked.

"Still with the kid," said Comet.

"What? You didn't get him first!" I shouted.

"He specifically told us to rescue you in case something happened to him," said Larry.

"Whatever," I said. "What I want to know is how'd you find me?"

Blitzen pointed to Larry. "The freak's horns. If you hadn't noticed, they're basically a Bobbie detector."

"See," said Larry. "I have skills."

I looked at the clock. "But there's no time. What did you expect—"

"You have to come with us to the North Pole now!" said Dasher. "You're our only hope to stop the Watcher!"

I shook my head. "But the Kill Switch! I threw it away."

Dasher rolled his eyes. "I am Larry. Hear me bore."

I looked to my dad, unconscious against the wall. Then I looked to the old photo of him with Uncle Dale. I at least had to try.

You can't matter if you don't try.

I turned to the reindeer. "Got room for two more in that sleigh?"

Chapter Twenty-Eight

Dad's watch read 11:58 as we crossed the Trans-Dimensional Boundary and the gross smell of refried beans head-butted its way into my nose. Below us a dense fog bank covered the North Pole.

If I did my trans-dimensional math right, I figured we had maybe thirty minutes to get inside Santa's workshop and shut down the Watcher before Christmas was destroyed forever.

No pressure.

We arrived at the North Pole to the sight of two tiny

dots waving frantically from the sleigh landing strip. I figured it had to be Gumdrop and Phil. I ordered Larry to land. Which he did. Sort of.

I dug myself out of the snow and started running toward Phil and Gumdrop only to discover . . .

It was too late. I looked up and saw . . .

The situation reminded me of that famous movie about that unsinkable ship that turned out to be mostly sinkable. As the ship's stern rose out of the water just before it sank, the main character said, "This is bad."

I always thought that was a really stupid thing to say. Until now.

One of the EWAs said, "For violating the laws of the North Pole you will be processed and taken to the Great Figgy Pudding Swamp for disposal along with the other human."

"The other human!" I cried. "Uncle Dale?!"

"They snagged him right after you left," said Phil.

"He put up quite a fight," added Gumdrop, "but they overpowered him."

"And now they're going to drop us into that dessert death trap too!"

Okay. I'd come a long way. I'd dealt with some seriously strange stuff. But after all this there was no way I would let Uncle Dale and me drown in a swamp of gross, stupid pudding.

"We've got to do something!" I whispered.

"But what?" said Phil.

Another EWA yelled, "On the ground NOW!"

"On the ground?" I said.

I looked at Phil and Gumdrop and whispered, "Snow angels!"

Phil and Gumdrop looked at me like I was crazy. Maybe I was. Or maybe . . . what was it Uncle Dale said? Maybe I've just seen stuff most folks wouldn't believe.

"Follow my lead," I said as I lay down flat on my back.

"Bobbie, this is a really bad idea," said Phil.

"You've got a better one?"

Gumdrop raised his hand. "I was a big fan of the whole immediate surrender thing."

"Too late. Get flappin'!" I said.

As we frantically waved our arms back and forth, the EWAs started getting itchy. It was now or never.

"NOW!" I yelled.

Phil, Gumdrop, and I all jumped up to the sight of . . .

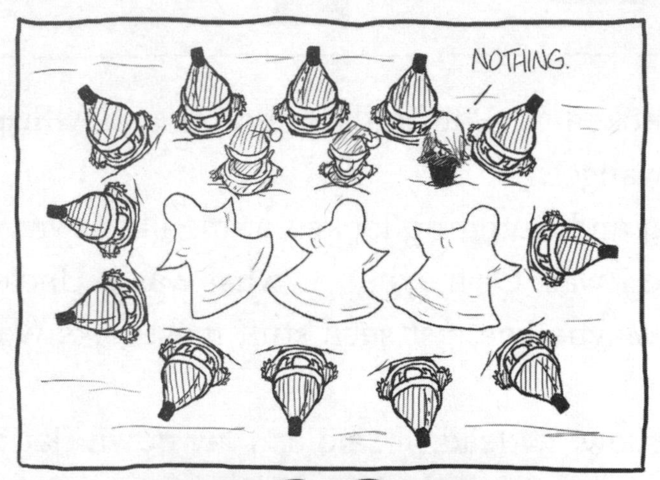

RUMBLE RUMBLE
ZING!

"DUCK!" yelled Gumdrop.

In the chaos, we made a break for it. I ran faster than I'd ever run before. Phil and Gumdrop tried to keep up.

"But the Watcher is the other way!" said Phil.

"We've got to free Uncle Dale!" I cried.

Gumdrop yelled, "We don't have time!"

"We're almost to the grove," I said.

"Look out!" yelled Phil.

This was it. We were done for. I could feel my heart skip a beat as the icy wings of the snow angels reached out to flash freeze my soul so they could savor it as a frozen tasty treat for all eternity.

Snow angels have some serious issues.

“Take cover, grunts!” boomed a familiar voice.

I looked up and what to my wondering eyes should appear but an angry snowman and several highly trained marine mammals. Oh, dear!

One of the snow angels reached for me just as the searing heat from General Frostman's angel duster hit it dead-on.

As I kicked melted snow angel off my shoes and checked to make sure Phil and Gumdrop were okay, I heard a cry.

It was Uncle Dale! We had to get him out! I started to charge into the dense missile-toe thicket when Phil tackled me from behind.

"It's too late!" said Phil. "We'll never get there in time!"

"But we can't just let him drown!" I shouted.

"We have to save Christmas!" cried Phil.

I got in Phil's face. "Christmas without my Uncle Dale isn't Christmas. I'm going in!"

Gumdrop pointed toward the remaining EWAs gunning for us. "Whatever you do, you need to do it now!"

I turned to the Missile-Toe grove. I could see Uncle Dale about fifty yards away slowly sinking in the sugary swamp. What I needed was wings. Wait!

I had an idea. Not my best idea. But with some luck and a steady seal it just might work.

I turned to Gumdrop and Phil. "Do you trust me?"

Phil looked at Gumdrop. "Do we have a choice?"

"No," I said as I turned to Blutarski. "You're taking us up. All of us. Now."

Blutarski saluted, hooked us up, and took off. The missile-toe plants must have sensed the threat, because they immediately began firing.

Yet somehow, with all the grace of an elephant swinging on a trapeze, Blutarski dipped and dove, barely avoiding the rain of flaming Yule logs.

"Get me lower!" I shouted.

We were almost to Uncle Dale, but he was sinking fast. His head was barely visible!

"Gumdrop! Phil!" I yelled. "One of you grab my feet! Blutarski, whatever you do don't fly away until I tell you to!"

"No, Bobbie," yelled Uncle Dale. "I don't matter! Save Christmas, not me!"

He was wrong. He did matter. He mattered to me and to my dad and mom and Tad!

He was almost completely under—his right arm and his mouth the only things sticking out of the black pudding. We were almost to him.

"Blutarski! Lower!" I shouted.

I kept my eyes fixed on Uncle Dale's outstretched hand as Blutarski flew me lower. This was it . . . One shot! I was laser focused and ready. But just as I was almost there I heard Gumdrop shout, "INCOMING!"

One second he was there, and then he wasn't.

"Let me go! I can save him!" I yelled.

"It's too late!" shouted Phil. "Any part of you gets stuck in that swamp and you're as good as gone too."

As I hung upside down the only thing I could see through my tears were the faded words my mom wrote on my cast earlier. . . .

That was it!

I screamed, "Blutarski! One more try!"

"But Bobbie!" cried Phil.

"Just trust me!" I yelled.

Blutarski lowered back to the place where Uncle Dale had last been.

"Get me closer!" I yelled.

I stuck my arm and cast into the dark swamp. For a brief moment I felt nothing but the thick, sugary pudding closing in around my cast. But then . . .

We had him! Uncle Dale was rising out of the swamp. Then . . .

Phil let go of one of my legs and reached down and grabbed Uncle Dale's other hand. NOW we had him.

"Blutarski! GO!" I screamed.

As Blutarski pulled up and away, I watched in slow motion as my hot pink cast slowly sank under the brown, sugary surface.

I flexed my fingers and wrist on my now cast-free hand. "Good thing I heal quickly."

We saved Uncle Dale. And with a whole three minutes trans-dimensional time left to save Christmas.

Again, no pressure.

Chapter Twenty-Nine

The problem with deciding that you can make a difference is that you actually have to make a difference. Deciding to do something isn't the same thing as actually doing it. It's just a start.

We had to finish what we started.

We still faced insurmountable obstacles. We had to destroy the Watcher. There was no time. And we were relying on the shaky reliability of a command-challenged cow out of water.

We were doomed. Again.

And yet I didn't feel doomed. I felt a calm confidence. Just put one foot in front of the other. Step by step . . . until the deed is done.

Step one: land on the workshop roof.

Okay, forget about step one.

Step two: enter the workshop.

Forget about step two. In fact, no more steps. Steps are for losers. It's time to improvise.

"I'm tired of these robo-rejects!" yelled Phil. "Bobbie, you go down the chimney while Gummy and I hold down the fort."

"And how might we accomplish that, Philip?" asked Gumdrop.

Phil held out his hands. "May I have this dance?

I was momentarily distracted by the elite elf martial arts on display (elite elf martial arts have that effect), when Uncle Dale yelled, "TWO MINUTES!"

We ran to the chimney. Uncle Dale hoisted me over the edge.

"What's to say this doesn't lead to a pit of snakes or a kiddy pool full of piranhas?" I asked.

"Guess we'll find out!" Uncle Dale said.

Then he dropped me Santa-style down the chimney. Sliding down chimneys was a rush! How could Santa prefer going through the front door?

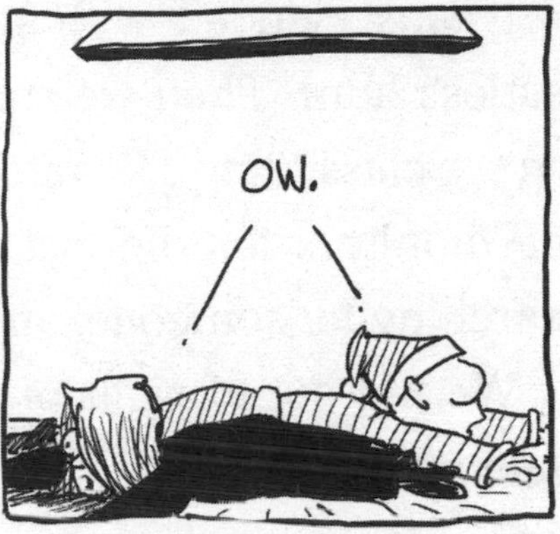

Oh, that's why.

"We've got to hurry!" shouted Dale.

We pulled ourselves together and charged into the Watcher's control room.

It was clouded with steam and vibrated with a restless hum. Then we saw the eye. It was calculating . . . classifying . . . watching. Frantically searching the monitors for the last naughty child. Frantically searching for someone, anyone . . . me.

We hid out of sight of the Watcher's gaze. Uncle Dale pointed to the eerie green glow of one of the monitors. "Oh no . . . It's listing every child in the world as naughty. The Watcher's not just destroying Christmas . . . it's destroying cheer, magic, good tidings . . . EVERYTHING!"

"What does that mean?!" I whispered.

"Without any cheer, there's no way to cross the Trans-Dimensional Boundary. We'll be stuck here forever!" he said.

That was not going to happen. First of all, I was tired of the cold and snow. Second, reindeer and elves are fun and all, but they're just so needy. And third of all . . .

Uncle Dale nodded. "Then let's shut 'er down."

"Nothing is happening!" I cried.

I hit the button again and again. Was it broken? Is this the wrong Kill Switch?! That's when a dialogue box popped up on the screen.

"Noooooo!" I cried.

I looked up at the clock. There were only forty-five seconds left! Uncle Dale shook his head.

"That's it," he said. "It's over."

I looked at Uncle Dale. "I'm the last nice kid!"

I thought about Tad . . . his favorite day gone. I thought about Dad decorating his tiny apartment to remind him of his family. I thought about Uncle Dale, who'd apparently been through this before. I thought about Mom and the locket she'd re-gifted to me. I felt for it around my neck and . . .

I picked the locket up and opened it.

I took a deep breath.

"HEY, WATCHER!" I shouted.

Uncle Dale looked at me. "What are you doing?!"

"Giving the Watcher something to watch."

"Bobbie! No!"

Metal gears whined and hydraulic pumps hissed

as the Watcher shifted his all-seeing eye toward the sound of my voice.

"So you know who I am, huh?" I hissed.

The Watcher responded in a hollow robotic voice: "You are naughty. No Christmas for you. You are NAUGHTY!"

"Don't you see, you're destroying Christmas! You're destroying cheer!"

"We cannot destroy. Only protect. We are the Watcher. We watch to protect."

"You watch. But you don't see. Naughty is sometimes nice, and nice is sometimes naughty. And YOU can't tell the difference."

"We must watch! We must watch! WE MUST WATCH!"

The clock was almost at midnight. It was now or never.

For a brief, almost imperceptible second, the eye of the Watcher twitched. It saw its own reflection in the locket. It saw its own actions. It saw . . .

. . . it was not nice. It saw . . .

. . . it was naughty.

Hundreds, thousands of images began to flash on the computer screen (and flash off the Naughty List).

The Watcher began to belch and hiss, rattle and prattle as rivets gave way and steam shot out in every direction.

"It's working!" said Uncle Dale.

"What do we do now?" I yelled.

Uncle Dale pushed me toward the door. "RUN!"

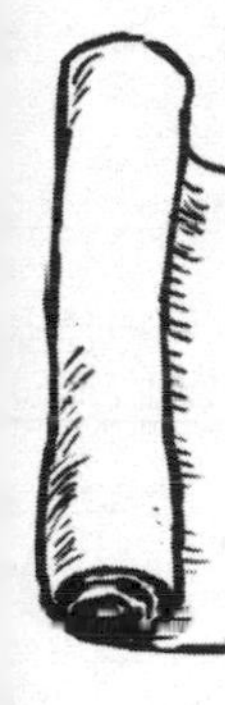

Chapter Thirty

There's this one part in the beginning of *Ninja Santa 5: Electric Boogaloo* where Ninja Santa's trying to save this elf resort in Barbados with a huge fund-raiser/ fireworks show. But the evil developer (who's trying to get rid of the resort) has hidden a propane tank next to all the fireworks. Nobody except Ninja Santa notices when the evil developer lights the fuse. Santa shouts "RUNNNNN!!!!!" really loud, and all the elves at the resort sprint in super slow motion as the explosion barely misses them. There's awesome music playing and everyone looks really, really cool.

This was not like that.

However, as the smoke finally cleared, I noticed that Uncle Dale and I were both still alive. So there's that.

It was just past midnight. We'd destroyed the Watcher, but had we saved Christmas?

I heard a whirring sound. And then a familiar laugh.

Santa smiled. "Wow. I guess you really do matter."

"You escaped!" I exclaimed. "How?"

"With a little help from my new favorite fashion accessory," he said, looking at Uncle Dale.

Santa handed Dale back his spaghetti strainer.

"Told ya! One size fits all!" said Uncle Dale.

"But what about the elves and the reindeer?" I asked.

"What about us?" yelled a high-pitched voice.

I turned around to the arrival of Santa's sleigh driven by Phil and Gumdrop and attended by all nine reindeer.

All the former EWAs, now free of the Watcher's robotic enslavement, gathered around the sleigh.

"You did it, Bobbie!" Phil cheered.

"We always knew you could," added Gumdrop.

My dad was curled up in the back of the sleigh, still unconscious.

"Is he okay?" I asked.

"Okay? Why, he's more than okay! He's the first gift of Christmas this year," said Santa.

Dasher gave Larry the stink eye. "Though you might want to put an ice pack on his noggin once you get home."

I smiled. "You mean . . . I got my wish? He's coming home?"

"It wasn't just your wish, Bobbie. Tad, your uncle, and your mom all wanted him home."

I looked down at my reflection in my locket and grinned. "And the Naughty List is no more," I said to Uncle Dale.

"Thanks to you, kiddo," he said.

"What really happened when you were a kid?" I asked. "Dad said they found you in your closet covered in snow?"

"Where you succeeded . . . I failed."

"You didn't fail, Dale," Santa said. "It was my fault."

"Dale did the best he could, but it wasn't enough. We returned him to his closet, where his family found him," said Santa.

I turned to Uncle Dale. "All these years, you thought you'd failed."

Dale shrugged. "I was a little kid. Stuff that happens to you when you're little sticks with you."

"Well, you didn't fail," I said. "We BOTH succeeded. What we do matters!"

Santa climbed into the sleigh as the elves packed it with presents. He pointed to Uncle Dale and me. "It's not a merry Christmas just yet. We've still got work to do."

"We?" Uncle Dale and I asked at the same time.

"Yep. We need all your cheer to help these reindeer fly double time. Now let's go!"

Uncle Dale and I climbed into the sleigh. Santa handed me the reins. "Care to do the honors?"

I looked at Uncle Dale, Phil, Gumdrop, and finally my sleeping dad.

"You can do this," said Santa.

"You're right. I can do this," I said.

Chapter Thirty-One

I awoke in the dark. My head hurt . . . really hurt . . . a professional-cage-fighter-just-punched-me-in-my-brain hurt.

I sat up. I was wet. Wait. I haven't wet the . . . No. There was fur everywhere. Oh, right . . . the reindeer. And the wetness must be from melted snow. I guess Santa just dumped me . . .

"MOM! Can I come downstairs yet?" shouted an excited voice.

It was Tad. I was home! In Tad's closet?

I peered through the slats in the door. Tad stood rocking from one foot to the other wearing one of his Santa suits. There was a thin residue of blue ink still on his face.

"Where's your sister? She's not in her room!" shouted my mom from the hallway.

"C'mon, Mom!" yelled Tad. "It's been Christmas for, like, six hours and forty-seven minutes already!"

Six hours and forty-seven minutes to deliver presents to the entire world. On trans-dimensional time, of course.

I stepped out of the closet. "Hey, squirt."

Tad stepped back. "Were you in there all night? That's really weird. Even for you."

Uncle Dale looked at me. "Oh . . . I was . . . just . . . checking to see if there was a portal to another dimension in here," he said.

Mom stared at Uncle Dale.

"Nope," Uncle Dale added, "this one's closed for Christmas."

"We're all here!" yelled Tad, running out of his room. "We can start!"

Uncle Dale and I followed Tad. I turned to Mom. "I guess it'll take a while to get the blue out."

"Yes. The dye-pack explosion was unfortunate. I don't know why you didn't just tell us you'd won the 3D Mega Machine."

"Won it?"

Uncle Dale poked me and whispered, "You're going to pay a couple of elves back for a *long* time."

"See? I knew Bobbie loved Christmas!" said Tad.

Mom rushed ahead to stop us at the bottom of the stairs. She smiled. "Okay, you guys . . . I have a big Christmas surprise for you. Are you ready?!"

"Yeah!" yelled Tad.

She gestured to the living room. "Okay, go ahead."

"SANTA!!!" yelled Tad as he ran outside.

We followed Tad outside.

"It *is* Santa!" yelled Tad.

We all looked up.

What was he doing with Dead-eyed Zombie Santa?

"I saw this old thing just sitting in the trash," said Dad. "I couldn't resist patching him up and putting him back in his proper spot. What do you think?"

With my dad standing next to him, Dead-eyed Inflatable Zombie Santa never looked so good.

"It's perfect," I said.

"Did Santa bring you home?" Tad yelled. "He did, didn't he? Of course he did! He got my letter! He *is* real! See, Bobbie? I told you he was real!"

"You were right, buddy," I said.

"Or you could say Santa found him a really cheap last-minute flight," said Mom.

Dad looked a little dazed. "Yeah. Right. A last-minute flight."

Out of the corner of my eye I saw the gnomes from the Christmas tiki display next door. Did one of them just blink? Gumdrop? Phil?

"I say it's magic!" cheered Tad.

"Maybe," Dad said. "But magic's not going to tie this Santa to the roof. I'm going to need a—"

And that's when I realized that Christmas isn't about elves and reindeer and Santa. It's not about magic. It's about what's real. And about sharing what's real. Together. Because in the end . . .

The End

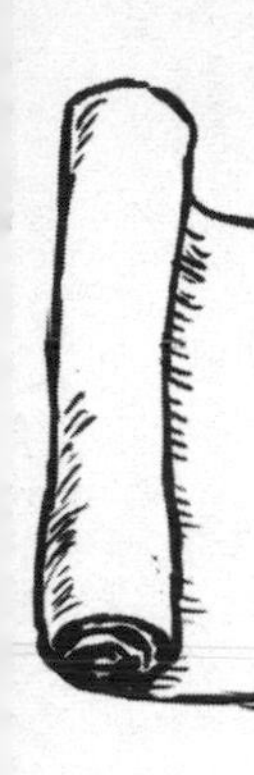

Acknowledgments

We'd like to thank everyone at HarperCollins for taking a risk on our attempt at seasonal silliness. Especially Nancy Inteli, our patient, enthusiastic editor (and lover of multiple exclamation points), her awesome assistant, Nicole Hoff, and the hardest working art director in publishing: Rick Farley. Also a big thank you to our agent, Dan Lazar, who championed *The Naughty List* from the beginning. To friends and family, we apologize for ruining Christmas by making it a year-round obsession with dumb questions like, "Would an incontinent reindeer say that?" and "How many speeds should a Spartan snowman semiauto hair dryer have?"* It's been a long, strange, jolly trip made special by the work and patience of you all. Thank you again.

*Low, Medium, and Melt

ABOUT THE CREATORS

Bradley Jackson's favorite Christmas gift was an Ultimate Warrior action figure his brother gave him. He is also a writer/filmmaker whose debut feature film *Intramural* was released by MGM/Orion Pictures. He is a co-owner of the production company Ralph Smyth Entertainment in Los Angeles, California. *The Naughty List* is his first book. Follow him on Twitter @bradleyjackson.

Michael Fry has been a cartoonist and writer for over thirty years. He has created or cocreated four internationally syndicated comic strips, including the current "Over the Hedge," illustrated by T. Lewis, which is featured in newspapers nationwide and was adapted into the hit animated movie of the same name. In addition to working as a cartoonist, Mike was a cofounder of RingTales, a company that animates print comics for all digital media, and he is the author and illustrator of the middle grade novel series The Odd Squad. He lives on a small ranch near Austin, Texas with his wife, Kim; their dog, Jack; and a dozen or so unnamed shrub-eating cows. Follow him on Twitter @MFryActual.